OUT FOR BLOOD

Craig had meant to go on up to MacQueen's from the turnoff at Territory Road, but it started to rain, and he headed the mile back to town, meaning to get a full meal under his belt and have his slicker if he was to go up on the mountain in a storm. He pulled into the livery stable, seeing Harry Fields turn from the rear and come running up the row of softly snorting, stamping animals.

"If you'll give Pepper and Salt something to eat, Harry, I'll be back in an hour."

"Doc, Doc, you got to git out of town quick," broke in Fields.

Craig had stood on the footboards to climb down off the buckboard, but he checked himself there, something chilling the very pit of him. "Why, Harry?"

"Jada MacQueen's boy has died, and Jada is down off the mountain, hunting for you."

COFFIN GAP

LES SAVAGE, JR.

LEISURE BOOKS   NEW YORK CITY

A LEISURE BOOK®

November 1999

Published by special arrangement with Golden
West Literary Agency.

Dorchester Publishing Co., Inc.
276 Fifth Avenue
New York, NY 10001

ISBN 0-8439-4632-6

EDITOR'S NOTE

The author's title for this novel was *The Doctor at Minnetaree.* Far more than the title had to be changed before it could be published as a book. There were restrictions in 1949 on who could be married to whom in a Western story and to deal as the author dealt with the theme of contamination, biological and environmental, was deemed both controversial and wrong-headed. The result of the severe editing to which the original manuscript was subjected produced a story so innocuous that it could be used as the basis for the Gene Autry movie, *Hills of Utah* (Columbia, 1951). *Coffin Gap* appears now for the first time as the author intended it should be published.

Chapter One

No one actually knew how Coffin Gap had come to be named. Some old mossy horns claimed it was due to the Minnetaree burial grounds up in Kootenai Cañon, though these Indian graves were hardly coffins as white men knew them but rather willow racks, holding their mordant burden of decaying bodies high in the cottonwoods that overlooked Territory Road where it ran through the cañon. Then there were other men who claimed the name had arisen from the number of killings the town had known. This was more logical, perhaps. It was as wild a boomtown as any. It could stand up, drink for drink, whoop for whoop, killing for killing, to Deadwood or Dodge or any other town with hair on its chest, from the Gulf to Canada.

Standing at the second story window of his office, Alan Craig watched the woman turn into Cutbank Street off Territory Road. She was driving her cut-under mountain wagon so hard it slued in the turn, splashing Montana mud thick as chocolate up over the pair of shaggy cow ponies that stood at the tie rack in front of the barber shop. The two men walking toward these animals from the harness shop stopped when they saw it happen. The woman's glance crossed theirs for just a moment as she passed them. Craig felt his own body draw up in sympathetic reaction to the strange tension of it.

Then the woman had hauled her wagon into the curb, calling to the barber as he came to his doorway, wiping his hands on his apron. His head turned part way toward those two cowhands, before he answered her. She spoke again, and, though the words were unintelligible to Craig, he could hear the sharp, angry tone of her voice. The barber faced back toward her, raising his arm to point at the window in which Craig stood.

The woman shook out her reins and trotted the nervous, lathered team to the tie rack before this building.

Craig guessed what was coming, had already turned down his cuffs and buttoned them, and was slipping into his coat when the knock came at the door. He opened it for her and stepped back. She entered with the same sense of nervous restraint the horses had imparted, and the impression of her this close struck him with palpable impact — the abundance of auburn hair, blown wild by the wind, the rich, creamy texture of flesh forming the finely chiseled planes of her face, the subtle, tantalizing fluctuation of green and violet and blue in the depths of her wide, candid eyes.

"You're the new doctor?" she asked.

"Alan Craig," he nodded.

A hesitation caught her, shadowing her face for a moment, bringing the start of a frown. Then she said: "I'm Garnet MacQueen. My little brother's pretty bad, up on the mountain. Would you come?"

He dipped his head in agreement, getting the small, black traveling bag off the floor, his flat-topped Stetson from a shelf. When he turned back, she was still standing there, studying him with that mixture of emotions in her face.

"What is it?" he asked.

"Have you got a gun?"

He met her eyes a moment longer. There was no question in his eyes, only a blank, withdrawing expression that seemed to hold something far removed from the present. Then he set the bag on the single chair in the meagerly furnished room, walked to the old roll-top desk, opened the top right-hand drawer, and took out a holstered Remington, unwrapping the belt to slip it under his coat tails and buckle it in front.

"Satisfied?" he asked.

Her smile, coming wryly, impulsively, was tempered by the

puzzled frown that followed it. Then she turned to go back out. Perhaps it was that her face had held him till then, directing his attention from the rest of her. Now this motion caught his eye. He had never seen so much made of a simple gingham dress. She was ripe through the breast and hips, with an early maturity, and the patterned cloth drew taut over each curve, as it came into contact, with a sibilant adherence.

Craig saw that the barber still stood in his doorway when they reached the mountain wagon. There was something almost painful to the carefully reserved neutrality in his face. This was not so of the cowhands. They stood by those horses with the Coronet brand now, and, as the woman shook out her reins, moving her team out into the street, Craig could not miss the vague, tight hostility in their faces. After the buckboard had passed them, he saw one lean over to say something in the other's ear, then turn to step aboard his horse, wheeling it about and cantering for an alley leading southward off Cutbank.

"Would it have been dangerous for your father to send one of his miners for me?" Craig asked the woman.

Her oblique glance held the beginnings of surprise. This altered to comprehension, filled with that wry, almost apologetic humor of which she seemed so capable.

"I wondered why you didn't ask me about the gun," she said. "I didn't think you'd been in town that long."

"Long enough to get some of the story," said Craig. "Your father's hydraulic operations are filling the river with so much débris it's polluting all the water down here and covering the valley with so much silt a lot of grazing land has been ruined."

"That's right." Her voice held acid, sarcastic acceptance. "Of course, they didn't tell you how many times Dad has tried to work out some plan with them that would solve the problem."

"No," he agreed. "They didn't."

"It would be very simple," she said bitterly. "If Dad wasn't such a stubborn, prejudiced old fool and the rest of them weren't such greedy, small-minded land-grabbers, all they'd have to do is choose one watercourse . . . just one near enough to his diggings so that he could channel the débris down it and into the Kootenai south of the basin. But every time one's suggested, it cuts across someone's land in the valley. Last time it was the Coronet. Fisher River only cuts through a hundred acres of their holdings, land that's already covered five feet with silt anyway, but Bowie French couldn't lose his precious, useless hundred acres."

"Bowie French?"

Her face turned part way toward him at the tone of his voice. "Yes. He's Coronet."

His chin had risen with his voice, and he let it drop back, that blank, withdrawing look robbing his eyes of focus. "Yes," he said. "I suppose so." He sat in silence for a moment, with the dim clatter of cogs and axle beneath him. "Feelings pretty bitter," he said at last.

"Killing bitter," she answered.

This time it was he who looked at her, surprised by the savagery of her voice. She drove on, refusing to answer his attention, and finally he settled back in the seat, relaxing the long, neatly coupled lines of his body in his short, blue-serge coat and string tie. The hat brim cast a dim shadow across the reserved, bony force of his face with its tall, prominent temples and deep-set eyes. They were black eyes, almost opaque when no emotion stirred him like this, but the pinpoints of light in the pupils gave them a sense of some deep, potent concentration on life that was never quite still. Though he had shaved this morning, the prominent angle of his jaw still held the bluish sheen of a heavy beard that could never quite be erased.

This shine, so close to the shine of steel, shimmered faintly across the ripple of jaw muscles as they clamped his teeth together in the irritation of seeing almost everyone along Cutbank turn to watch the wagon. This was Coffin Gap's main street, formed from a wagon road that came across Cutbank Bridge to cut the town in half, running east and west, to become a wagon road once more that wound through the rest of the fertile Cabinet Basin. Territory Road, originally part of the old Tobacco Plains Trail, came in from the south to enter Cutbank between First Street and the Kootenai River. Garnet MacQueen turned the wagon down here, passing into the older part of town. For a few blocks it was lined with early miners' shacks now lived in by the poorer families of town, a couple of rot-gut saloons with their windows boarded up, and the dilapidated hip-roofed barn Emanuel Beebe used for livery stables.

The MacBell House, standing gaunt and alone, the last building on Territory Road, had been the original stage station. Since the stageline had moved its offices into the center of town, someone had turned this place into a rooming house, building another story of frame atop the crusty, blackening logs of the earlier structure. Craig's body did not move in the seat, but his head turned slowly, as they went by, until he could turn it no more. Only when they were completely past, and he could not see it any longer without actually turning his body, did he allow his face to swing back to the front. The live, quickening little lights were still blotted out by some inner darkness, giving his eyes a somber, withdrawn expression. He made no attempt to veil it as he realized the woman's attention was on him. She said nothing, and they rattled by the turnoff to the Coronet, leaving it behind them, to bring the Fisher River into view ahead. It was a wild, tumbling watercourse, coming down from high in the Cabinets to join the Kootenai a mile to the east. The wooden bridge crossing the river seemed to tremble constantly with its vitality.

There was the fruity, earthy reek of flood water from the river swelling over its banks below, churned chocolate by its own turbulence. Craig could see the silt and débris of former years spread heavily over the bottom and into the down-sloping meadows on this side. They came in sight of a pocket where a house and corrals had stood. The building was up to its window sills in silt, and the only thing of the fences in sight was the very top of the posts, thrusting up from the dark muck. He made no attempt to hide the vague shock on his face, staring at this ruin. She met it with that acid, devilish sarcasm.

"Piles up a lot in seven years, doesn't it?"

Before he could answer, something ahead caught his eye, and he half stood in the seat to make it out. "Better pull down," he told her sharply. "A tree's fallen across the road."

Light made its fitful, auburn glint through her hair with the sharp lift of her head. Then she was sawing at the reins to halt the animals before they ran head-on into the poplar sunk deeply in the muddy ruts by some recent fall. Craig started to climb down, meaning to see if the shoulder would bear their passage, when the first rider appeared in the timber, sliding his little cow pony down a slushy cutbank to the road. Another man followed, and Craig lowered himself back into the seat. Neither of them was one of the cowhands who had been in town, but their horses bore the same brand: that small, distinctive crown on the rump.

The first man was on a blue-tick roan, sidling it in toward Craig's side of the buckboard. He was small and lean as rawhide, with a sense of incessant, sour calculation forming its countless tracks at the corners of his squinted eyes. A lustrous, russet beard covered all but a hint of the sharp belligerence of his jaw. It was the only clean, groomed thing about him. The rest was a faded, tattered ducking jacket of blue denim, brass-studded Levi's covered with stable filth and freshly splashed muck, and an old horse-thief hat so black with grease and dirt there was no telling its original color.

"Working for the Coronet now, Evan?" said Craig mildly.

"I didn't think you'd remember me, Alan," grinned Evan Fox.

"I haven't forgotten much, Evan," Craig said. "You've got a new saddlemate, though."

That took Evan Fox's squinted eyes momentarily to the second rider who had pulled his big, rawboned buckskin up by the opposite side of the rig, holding back a little in some deference to Garnet. He was a tall man, taller than Craig, reminding the doctor of a jayhawker somehow in his striped pants of another era, stuffed into the tops of muddy jackboots. His gun, slung in a slick, battered scabbard against one narrow hip, was as old as his pants, and as much used, one of the .36 caliber Navy revolvers put out during the Civil War. It held as much dour, somber threat as the man himself.

"That's Ingo Hubbard, Alan," Fox said. "Ingo, meet the new doctor of Coffin Gap."

Ingo tilted his head downward so that his two upraised fingers touched the hatbrim. "Pleased," he murmured laconically.

"Bowie French sent us, Alan," said Fox. "He'd like to have a little talk before you go up on the mountain."

"I'll have it after I come back," Craig told him. "A boy's sick up there."

"From what I hear, all MacQueen's boy has is another bellyache," Fox told him. "You know how kids are always getting bellyaches."

"It's more than that," Garnet put in hotly. "He's been having convulsions all day. If you'll move your horse, we can get around that tree on the shoulder."

"If you'll turn your wagon around, you can reach the side

13

road to the Coronet ranch back by the bridge," said Ingo Hubbard.

Craig felt his body lift up with the sharpness of his answer. Then he shut his lips on it, settling back against the seat with a careful, deliberate effort. "I know what Bowie wants to see me about, Evan," he told Fox. "You can tell him the same thing I would. This fight between you and the miners isn't my province. I won't take sides in it. My business is to heal sick people, no matter who they are."

Fox's double-rigged Nelson creaked faintly as he leaned forward to cross his arms over the slick horn and to bend over them. "How about the people who are hurt, Alan?"

"Hurt, sick, it's the same thing."

"Who'd heal you, Alan, if you were hurt real bad?"

Craig met Fox's eyes a moment before he spoke. "I'm disappointed in you, Fox," he said then. "I always thought it took a rather small man to waste his time with threats."

Meager reaction to this passed through Fox's eyes as he slipped one of his arms forward to put a hand on Craig's shoulder. "Turn the wagon around, Alan. We'll go back and see Bowie."

"Take the wagon on ahead, Garnet," said Craig.

He heard the woman's indrawn breath. There was a faint rustle of leather as she lifted the reins. Ingo Hubbard spurred his buckskin so that it came against the wagon broadside. He leaned out and grabbed the ribbons from Garnet's hands. Craig's violent motion came at the same time. It tore Fox's hand loose as the doctor whirled in the seat to lean across Garnet's lap.

Ingo thought Craig was reaching for the reins and lifted them high. Craig ignored them, yanking the buggy whip from its socket and bringing it up with a sweep of his arm. The lash struck Hubbard's face with a sharp, bitter crack. The man

14

shouted in pain, rearing back in his saddle. This brought the reins of his own horse up viciously. The beast pawed air, squealing wildly. Blinded by the whip, Hubbard could not keep his seat. He pitched off the back.

Craig whirled back toward Fox. The man's horse was dancing excitedly away from the wagon. Fox was fighting this and trying to get his gun out at the same time. Wanting to finish it completely, Craig dropped the whip and launched himself off the seat before Fox was out of reach. He struck the flank of the roan with one arm hooking about Fox's narrow waist. When Craig fell back from the animal, he pulled the man with him onto the ground.

They struck with the doctor on the bottom. The blow of it stunned him. He had enough presence of mind left to wrap his legs around Fox, grabbing for the gun wrist. With the sharp, bony feel of it in his fingers, Craig twisted hard. He heard Fox's grunt of pain, felt the heavy gun slip down between them from the man's helpless fingers. Fox tried to tear away from Craig. The doctor let him go just far enough for room to rise.

Fox was on his feet with the front wheel of the wagon behind him when Craig found his knees. He threw himself at Fox to pin him against the wheel. Here he hit him in the belly. Twice. With all the weight of his body behind each blow. Then he moved backward, getting off his knees onto his feet. Fox doubled over, hugging his belly with both arms, the jaundice of nausea staining his face as he fell forward into the mud.

Across the low bed of the wagon Craig could see that Ingo Hubbard had just gained his feet. He was turning so that he faced the doctor over the wagon. Craig had no conscious understanding of his own intent though all of Hubbard's tension seemed focused on the doctor's right hand, held in a stiff, curling way out to the side when Fox called in a sharp, painful voice: "Watch his gun, Ingo, watch his gun!"

Ingo Hubbard remained in that grotesque suspension of all motion, staring across the mountain wagon at Craig. The doctor could not count the expressions forming their mingled, shuttling pattern through that dour face. The savage intent seemed to fade before something else that came insidiously up from underneath. Finally, like the ebbing of a tide, the rigid tension left Ingo's right arm, and he dropped it carefully to his side.

"All right," he said sullenly. "I guess Bowie can tend to that."

Only then was Craig conscious of his own reactions. It had probably come in response to his first sight of Ingo across the wagon. His hand had pulled one side of his coat off the butt of his gun, to leave it free, and was still hovering over it in approximately the same position Ingo's hand held. *How strange,* Craig thought, *the way habit can cling.* He let his eyes remain on Hubbard a little longer. Then he turned toward Fox, who was still crouched on the ground, a pinched, unrelenting rage filling his narrow face.

"Bowie didn't tell you to do this," Craig said, half in question, half in statement. The man glared sourly at him, refusing to speak. "You tell him this, then," Craig said. "It's the same thing I told you. This fight between the valley men and Jada MacQueen isn't my business. You're going to get nothing but neutrality from me as long as I'm here. But that doesn't mean I won't fight anyone who tries to stop me from what *is* my business."

Chapter Two

As the road penetrated the mountains, it narrowed, following the Fisher River precariously up through deep, shadowed cañons, sometimes rising above it to dizzying shelves with the water no more than a silver flash through a mottled cloak of dark foliage far below, sometimes winding along so close to the edge that the wheels turned dark with the splashing they got. The untrammeled roar of that tumbling water was always with them, whether near, drowning out everything else, or distant, forming a subdued background for whatever other noise broke through.

The woman's concentration was upon guiding the steaming, laboring team up the grades. Finally, however, they were blowing so hard she had to halt the wagon. They were on a ledge of road, high above the river, and the two of them sat silently for a space, staring in mutual awe at the vast panorama plunging away beneath them. Craig could feel, though, in the small, restless shift of Garnet's body her attention changing to him.

"They were so afraid of your gun," she said at last.

He did not offer to answer, or to look at her. There was something unwilling in the set of his long, angular face, but she ignored it.

"I wondered why you didn't seem to question when I asked you about it in the office," she went on. "I thought it was because you knew how dangerous things had gotten in town. It was more than that, though, wasn't it? You don't question a thing that's natural to you. Like a person telling you it's cold outside, and you'd better put on your coat. It's that natural to you, isn't it?"

He still did not answer, and she gave an impatient little

17

shake at the reins. The horses stamped peevishly, blowing. She was frowning faintly now, recalling something.

"Alan Craig," she said softly. "I should have known, really, when I first saw your name on the door. It did puzzle me for a minute there in the office. I had the feeling I should know you. I guess I was too worried about my brother to follow it through. You left Coffin Gap nine years ago, didn't you? I was only thirteen at the time. I guess that's why it didn't make much impression on me. I used to see you in town once in a while, when we'd come down off the mountain for supplies. Bob Craig was your father, wasn't he? Ran the old Scissors spread. And Bowie French worked for him. And taught you how to use that gun."

"Yes," Craig said, speaking finally on a heavy, restrained breath. "Bowie French."

"That would make him a good friend, wouldn't it?" she asked.

"You don't get good with a gun in a few days," he told her. "Bowie rode for Dad a couple of years."

"Why was he so interested in teaching you that?"

"Bowie and I worked together a lot, out in the line camps. I guess Dad sort of put it in his head. Dad wanted me to have the ranch after him, and he said a man should be a master with all the tools of his trade. He was brought up in the old school. They figured a gun was just as important as a branding iron."

"Not such an old school," she said. There was something almost pensive in her voice for that moment. She seemed to lift herself from it with effort. "Didn't you want to be a cattle-man?"

"I wanted to be a doctor."

"Even then?"

"You know how kids are. I guess it started out just the way some kids want to be engineers, or sheriffs. But it got to be

18

more than that. That was Mother, I guess. She didn't want me to run cattle. She'd seen three generations of Craigs live and die in the bunkhouse, never getting above a thirty-and-found hand. Dad went broke in Texas three times trying to make a go of it. Then he drove a herd up the Chisholm into Wyoming and lost it in the winter of 'Seventy-Two. It broke his heart trying to get the Scissors started here. Ma's heart too, I guess. Not that she ever complained. It just put a craving, way down deep in her, for her son to get out of a business that would do that to a man."

"What changed you?" she asked. "You seemed pretty passionate in that defense of your right to doctor anyone who was sick back there with Evan Fox. What changed it from the way a kid wants to be an engineer or a sheriff into a true ideal?"

"I never thought of myself as an idealist."

She was frowning that way again, as if in more recollection. "Your father was killed the year you left, wasn't he? Did that have any effect?"

"On me?" He shrugged, smiling sadly. "If there has to be a turning point, I guess that was it. Dad was shot in the lungs out on the range."

Some strange alteration in the lines of her face as he said this caused Craig to stop. He turned toward her to surprise an expression in her eyes, as intense as it was indefinable. She lowered her glance quickly, looking at her tightly folded hands.

"You brought him into town?" she asked.

"Yes," he answered dubiously. "Coffin Gap wasn't much then, you remember. We got to the old MacBell House when Dad couldn't go any farther because the jolting of the wagon was hurting so much. I sat with him while someone went on in for a doctor. There wasn't any. And I remember the thing I kept thinking. . . ."

This brought the faces, somehow, burgeoning up out of the

past, like sallow, grotesque masks, bobbing about in the feeble illumination of the bull's eye lantern a hosteler had brought into the waiting room. Bearded, reeking miners, down off Mac-Queen's new hole up on the mountain or the other diggings that had already begun to peter out, and blinking, leathery cowhands from the few shoestring outfits trying to gain a toe-hold in the basin at the time. And the voice. It had been one of those cowhands. Timothy Dunnymead, from Henri Nassaur's Cocked Hat, saturated with that awful reek of the kinnikinnick he was always smoking.

"You won't find no doctor in this town, boy. That's one animal we ain't got."

And then his father's hand, seeking his, gripping it with surprising strength for a dying man, and the eyes, bright and clear in that last moment.

"You don't blame me for holding you back, do you, Alan? I would have sent you to that school sooner, if I could have gotten the money. I guess, in my heart, I hoped you'd forget about it, working with the cattle, and realize your place was here. But I did plan to help you, if you really wanted to go. I wish your mother had lived for this day, because now I see I was wrong. Some men was meant to get big with cattle, but not the Craigs. I won't hold you back any longer, will I, Alan? What we've got in the Scissors ought to fetch enough money for your start. Use it right, Alan, the way you've wanted to, the way your ma wanted you to!"

But somehow Alan Craig's mind had not been on the words, or what they could mean to him. It was filled with one thought. *If there had been a doctor here, this wouldn't have happened.* Not whether some high-line rider down out of the Missions had done this, or a man following his father up from Texas for some old vengeance. Only that one thought.

"If there had been a doctor here, this wouldn't have happened. . . ." Craig felt his whole body twitch faintly as he realized the thought had been formed into sound, the sound of his own voice saying it, not in the past, but in the present, with this woman sitting beside him. He turned apologetically to her, filled with the disturbing sensation of having been gone a long time. But she was studying him with a strange, deep sympathy in her face.

"You loved your father very much, even though he blocked your way?"

He realized what was on her mind, and shook his head. "He never really blocked it. We never clashed over it. He just didn't understand, until the very last. I . . . I thought a lot of Dad."

"More than you can put into words?"

He glanced at her, surprised by her insight. "Yes," he said in a vague discomfort. "I guess you're right."

"And his death made a very deep impression on you."

He stared beyond her, filled once more — as he always was when memory of his father came — with the realization of just how deeply that impression extended. "I'll never forget it," he murmured at last.

"I wonder," she said, in a soft, husky way, "just how many people in Coffin Gap will understand that in you."

She gazed a moment at his face. Then she shook the reins out, and turned her attention to the animals. The country they had passed through was familiar to Craig, from the time he had driven Scissors' beef up here for summer pasture. But they were coming now into a land he had never seen. A land of vast, pristine silence, broken infrequently by the call of some wild thing, or the tumbling crash of mountain water down a rocky defile, or a greater sound, like the roll of surf on a distant shore, when the wind filled the top foliage of tamarack and pine.

Adits were beginning to scar the face of the slope — the gaping mouths of tunnels used in the earlier lode mining, before

21

the veins pinched out. They had been out of sight of the Fisher for some time, but, dropping down a steep, shelved grade, they came to the broad floor of a cañon through which the upper reaches of the river flowed. And to the first sluice. It appeared on the slopes near the head of the cañon, writhing down out of timber like a great, disjointed snake. It passed above the road on a high wooden trestle, dropping down off the other side till its end opened into the river below, the whole structure trembling with the constant passage of water and gravel and débris. Craig could see the filthy muck spouting from its mouth into the river, dumping uncounted tons into the water every hour. He was aware of Garnet's expectant, sardonic attention on him, and he felt the tension driving its wedge between them. He offered no comment, and neither did she.

The road turned to follow the line of the sluice through that timbered head of the valley, breaking free of the trees at last to come within sight of the hydraulic crews. There was something awesome — and something pathetic, too — about that puny, ant-like group of men in their running, shouting, hectic attack on the mountain. There must have been a dozen of them around the three great, brass nozzles set up on tripods. The streams of water from these formed white plumes that bit into the gravel and rock of the slope with a vicious, splattering roar. For a moment Craig lost that sense of tension, staring in frank amazement at the scene.

"I had no idea it was on such a vast scale," he said.

"What?" she asked.

He raised his voice to be heard above the thunderous sound. "When I left, they were doing it with pans and Long Toms."

"Do you blame Dad for fighting so hard? Every cent he's got in the world is invested here."

"Those nozzles look like they pack a wallop."

"More than you can imagine. One of our men got his shovel

22

caught in a stream of water last year. It broke both his arms."

"What about those men on the flume?"

"That's the upper end of the sluice we've been following," she said, a shy, hesitant pride lighting her eyes at his interest. "You can see that wing dam just below where the nozzles are dumping the gravel into the river. The dam diverts the river into the sluice. As the water and gravel are washed down, the gold sinks to the bottom and is caught in riffles."

"While the rest of the muck goes right back to the river," he said, unable to contain the thought.

The momentary pride dropped away from her, and she turned to him in angry defense. "There isn't any place else for it to go. It wouldn't do any good to try and carry it away from the river in a valley this narrow. Wherever we dump the stuff, it would pile up and eventually find its way back to the lowest point, or be carried into the river by the spring floods. You . . . oh . . . !"

She said the last in hopeless anger, turning away from him and venting her spite on the reins. He stirred uncomfortably, sorry he had made an issue of it. He could not help notice it on every hand, however, as they drove on up the river, miles of slope where this whole side of the mountain had been literally dumped into the Fisher. Finally they began to climb a shelving road to a broad plateau with the first buildings in sight, a pair of long, rude bunkhouses, built half way up with undressed logs, topped with canvas.

From between these cabins a man came. He was not running fast. But there was some frightened purpose to the unremitting jog trot that brought the doctor forward on the seat to stare at him. Not until Craig saw the eyes did he recognize the fellow. They were immense, sloth-like in their protuberant luminosity, blinking constantly, as if the light bothered them.

Garnet halted the wagon as the man reached them. He

stopped near the seat, grasping its edge with a hand swollen and gnarled by a lifetime of labor. He stared up at the doctor for a moment, frowning with recognition.

"You really come back," he said.

Craig nodded, smiling dimly. "How's the rheumatism, Jack?"

"No good. If Jada'd quit this fool washing and get back to stoping, I'd have no more trouble. . . ." Cousin Jack halted himself abruptly, his heavy, bulldog jaws clamping shut so hard over the words that Craig could hear the click of teeth. When he spoke again, it was to Garnet, though he still held Craig with those eerie, blinking eyes. "You'd better not take him on up, Garnet. After you left, one of the men came back from Brockhalter's. Word had reached there that the new doc was a Craig. Jada almost went crazy. He's got himself barricaded in the house with a gun, and nobody can get to him. Says he'll shoot anyone that tries it."

"He'll let me in," Garnet told him. "Climb aboard, Cousin Jack, if you're going."

The man was small and wiry, in nothing but an undershirt and a pair of stag pants, wet to the knees. Hard ridges of muscle rippled beneath his grimy skin as he hoisted himself over the side without much effort, to squat in the bed behind the seat.

It bothered Craig to have him back there, out of sight. He could not forget those huge, blinking eyes. When Cousin Jack had first appeared in Coffin Gap with MacQueen, his name had caused everybody to take him for a Cornishman, for that was what many of the Cornish miners were called. It had been popular opinion that Jack's eyes were a racial inheritance from the centuries the Cornishmen had spent underground mining their tin, until darkness was more their element than light. Craig realized the fallacy of that now. In the first place Jack was not Cornish, but an itinerant Yankee miner who had spent his

24

apprenticeship in the mines of Cornwall and returned to the States with a taste for their pasty and Saffron bread. The condition of his eyes was probably due to goiter, or some allied condition. Yet, even with this knowledge based on his medical training, Craig still could not cast off the haunting spell of that earlier superstition. The man always conjured up a picture in his mind of a furry, repulsive, three-toed sloth, hanging from a branch and staring off into the night with those luminous, unworldly eyes.

Garnet reached the bunkhouses, circling around them to head toward a stand of spired pine. At the opposite edge of this stand, within the trees, a half dozen men were gathered, peering at a large, substantial log house that stood against the steep slope, across a broad, boulder-strewn meadow. The mark of their trade was on these men, grimed into their flesh and under their nails and in their hair, until they seemed a part of the earth itself. Most of them were still wet to the knees from hydraulicking, with drying mud caked on them above this. Craig felt like a traveler from another world under the hostile curiosity of their eyes. One of them disengaged himself from the group as the wagon pulled up, a tall, stooped man, wiping his hands nervously on a greasy apron.

"You better not go up there, Miss Garnet. Jada kicked me out of the house. He's up at that window with his over-and-under gun, and. . . ." He broke off to bend over in a wracking, hollow cough, the mark of the silicosis so many of these miners contracted. Garnet got down from the wagon and put her hand on his shoulder.

"Take it easy, Washoe. This is the doctor. Maybe he can do something for you, too. This is our cook, Alan. The miners' con caught him in the Comstock, and he hasn't been able to work below ground since."

The man had controlled his coughing by now and turned

25

his sallow, emaciated face up to stare at the doctor. "Alan Craig," he said, putting some curious significance into it with the inflection of his voice.

Before Craig could answer, Garnet turned to stare at the house. Then, without a word, she strode past the men and out into the open. Craig started to follow but had not yet emerged from the timber, when the shot crashed. Craig felt his whole body pulled upward with the shock of seeing the bullet kick up earth a few feet to the side of Garnet. She herself had stopped, her mouth open. Then a hot flush swept her face, and she cried up at the house: "Dad, it's me."

"I can see who it is!" The voice came from the house like a rumble in the mountain. "I'll shoot you or anybody else who tries to bring that Alan Craig in here. I'm not having a doctor for this kid, Garnet. I told you that."

Garnet shook her head. "I'm coming, Dad," she said, and started to walk forward once more. Halted by the shocking surprise of that first shot, Craig now made a second, belated start to catch up with her. But, before he was clear of the trees, another shot made its thundering explosion, the echoes clapping back and forth through the mountains in gigantic applause. Garnet took one more faltering step toward the house, then halted, to stare at it with a twisted face. Then she wheeled to stumble back into the trees, catching Craig before he was free of them. She faced in against the gnarled, ruddy corrugation of a pine trunk, blackened down one side by old-man's beard. Her shoulders formed a tense, high line, trembling with her angry sobs.

"The worst part is," she said in a small, strangled voice, "he's so capable of it." The movement of her shoulders ceased abruptly, and she whirled on the men savagely, face streaked with tears. "Well, so am I. Give me your gun, Doctor."

"Now wait a minute," he told her. "There must be some

other way. Is that the mouth of a tunnel just behind the house?"

"It's a part of the old Jada Hole," Washoe offered. "Jada had this mountain honeycombed with shafts before the vein pinched out, and he turned to hydraulicking."

"Would there be another way to get into that same tunnel without him seeing us?"

"There's an old adit below the bunkhouses," said Washoe. "Must be a dozen winzes connecting it with that tunnel behind the house."

Craig reached into the buckboard for his bag. "Can somebody take me?"

Cousin Jack caught his arm, a latent, crushing strength in the grip of his fingers. "Wait up. What do you mean to do?"

"Get in from behind," said Craig. "You talk with him out here and keep him at the front of the house."

"And if you do get in?"

Craig shrugged. "Whatever's necessary."

Cousin Jack's luminous eyes lowered to the brazen glint of shells in Craig's gun belt. "I don't think so."

"I do," said Garnet angrily. "Dad's a crazy, old fool, and he hasn't got any right to endanger Duncan's life like this. Let him go, Cousin Jack."

The man faced toward her without releasing Craig's arm. "Garnet, you know what Jada's capable of. He won't give up without a fight. Anything's liable to happen in there."

"Like Jada's getting shot?" said Garnet hotly. "I can't help it. He was willing to shoot me, wasn't he? Let him go, now, Cousin Jack, and stay out here and keep him busy. And if you let Jada know what we're doing, you won't have a job in these diggings past today. Count on that."

Sullenly, reluctantly, Cousin Jack let that hand slide off. Garnet inclined her head for Craig to follow her. Their feet made a sibilant, brushing sound in the carpet of russet pine

27

needles, following the timber around the bunkhouses to where the plateau sloped off sharply. They were out of sight of the log house when the mouth of another tunnel appeared. She led Craig into this with familiar ease, picking her way down the rusty tracks and around an old, high-sided ore car. He began to fumble for a match, and she must have heard him.

"We don't need a light," she said. "There's liable to be gas farther on."

After that was the darkness. He had never experienced such utter lack of light. It made him think of Cousin Jack's eyes, somehow, and wonder, wryly, if the man actually was capable of seeing in this. Her hand in his was warm, reassuring. Once she halted, and he came abruptly against the warmth of her hips. He felt the sharp breath lift her ribs, and wondered if it was the contact of their bodies. Then he realized his own breathing had accelerated.

They came to a ladder, and she guided him up. He realized this must be the winze Washoe had talked of, leading from this lower tunnel to an upper level. It seemed they turned back in the other direction. He could not be sure. Finally he thought he saw light again. It brought a breathless expectancy to him. In the foreign darkness, so conscious of her presence, their real purpose had been blocked from his thoughts. Now, however, it became uppermost, a keen, trembling anticipation, like a faint nausea at the pit of his stomach, the same feeling he had known back at the hospital before a major operation. They reached the end of the adit and were looking at the rear of the house, a hundred feet down the hill. From across the meadow they could hear Washoe calling to Jada, and the man's angry, roaring answer.

"There's a kitchen," Garnet told him in a hushed, tense whisper. "Then the bedroom Duncan's in. Dad's probably in the front room beyond, at the window." Her hand tightened on his, and her face turned up to him in a mute plea. "Doctor, please. . . ."

"Don't worry," he smiled. "I won't have to shoot him. The worst he can get is my gun barrel along the side of his head."

And what's the worst I can get? he wondered as he ran down the slope toward the rear door. It was unlatched, and he slipped into the kitchen. The floor was of unpainted, whipsawed lumber, and the logs themselves sufficed for the inside walls. An immense iron stove stood at one side with a sooty pipe going through the ceiling, and a pile of greasy dishes stood in a sink half filled with water. He put his bag on the sink and got out his Remington, pushing open the bedroom door softly.

The boy lay tangled up in a patchwork quilt and blankets, his curly, tousled head thrown back, eyes closed. His shallow breathing was the only sound.

"Stay back there, Washoe," Jada yelled from the front room "And tell that doc he might as well go back to town."

The boy did not open his eyes at the sound. Craig went past him softly. The door into the living room was part way ajar, and Craig had his first momentary view of Jada MacQueen before he spoke to the man. MacQueen had come up from the bottom of his profession, and it was stamped all over him. His beginnings lay in California in '49 with the pick and pan of those early days, coming up through the Chinese water wheel and the first crude sluice boxes, the rocker and cradle and the Long Tom, the thousand cave-ins of the coyoters when the first placering began, watching the hydraulic system develop from Chabot's canvas fire hose without any nozzle to the immense pressure systems he was using today.

MacQueen might have been one of those coyoters caught in a cave-in himself, for one side of his face had been crushed by some former accident, leaving an ugly depression of yellow, scabrous scar tissue and puckered flesh where the cheekbone should be. The rest of his face was not molded — it was hewn like a rough juxtaposition of granite slabs forced together, each harsh, battered plane of brow and jaw a vivid reflection of the primitive, brutal capacities of the man. He was an immense red-headed giant, with a great, beefy belly that filled his flannel shirt with no sense of fat, thrusting against his belt like a great, square keg. He had an over-and-under gun across the window and was staring out across the meadow in malevolent concentration.

"MacQueen," said Craig quietly, "I've got a revolver on you. Drop your gun to the floor before you turn around."

A hoarse grunt escaped MacQueen. He remained in that tense suspension for a space empty of sound. Then, slowly, he allowed the over-and-under to slide down off the sill. It made a sharp clatter against the whipsawed lumber, and then he turned to face Craig. For a moment all his weight was forward on his toes, and his little eyes glittered with the impulse to rush Craig, gun and all. Then he settled back, a guttural, animal sound coming from deep inside his chest.

"Alan Craig," he said in a hoarse, trembling voice.

Without answering, Craig called for Garnet to come in. There was the soft clatter of her feet on the boards through the kitchen, the bedroom. Then she must have been behind him, for MacQueen's eyes shifted that way, and his head lowered like a sulking bull's. "I should have shot you out there," he said.

"And you would, too, wouldn't you?" said Garnet hotly, moving around Craig.

"I sure would," shouted MacQueen, his voice swelling to that boreal rumble in a new burst of anger. "Ain't no daughter of mine that goes and gets a doc when I tell her not to. I'm not having it, Garnet, I tell you. That boy don't need a doctor any more than I do."

"All you've got to do is look at Duncan to see how bad he is," answered Garnet. "He's been vomiting for two days, Doctor, and this morning he was taken by convulsions."

"At least let me examine the boy, MacQueen," Craig suggested.

"Not a finger."

"Yes, he will!" cried Garnet, running forward. MacQueen made some turning motion to stop her, but she had reached his over-and-under too soon, scooping it up and raising it with the muzzle on him. Her auburn hair tossed with the jerk of her head toward the bedroom. "Now come in where we can watch you."

The expression in MacQueen's eyes was plain — a baffled inability to comprehend that his own daughter could do this.

"You'd do it to me, wouldn't you?" she asked. "I *am* your daughter, Jada, and I'm capable of just about anything you are."

As she said this, she lifted her head in a sharp, tossing motion. *Like a bridling horse,* thought Craig wryly. The deadly seriousness of it did not escape him, but it fascinated him, somehow, to see this bizarre clash between two such violent personalities. He turned into the bedroom then, pulling a chair from the foot of the bed to sit near the boy. Garnet followed, and MacQueen, standing over against the wall at her bidding, bending forward as if nothing but the most tenuous force were keeping him from their destruction.

There was a large swelling on one side of the boy's abdomen, and he moaned in his delirious stupor when Craig touched it. There was a pan beneath the bed, and the doctor moved it out with a foot, studying it.

"He's been vomiting fecal matter from the intestine," he told them. "It looks like intussusception."

"Don't give me none of them big words," said MacQueen.

31

"An intestinal obstruction."

"You mean his guts is clogged up? How could that be? He has an iron digestion, just like me."

What had occurred must have been apparent to the miners outside, for Washoe and Cousin Jack appeared in the doorway, pushed from behind by others. They stopped there when they saw Garnet holding the rifle. Craig's eyes had picked up the remains of a meal on the bedside table, and he nodded at the plate.

"What's that? Fried beef and potatoes?"

"Three times a day," said MacQueen. "Been feeding on it all my life without missing a meal and I never had a sick day. Ain't that right, Washoe?"

"Sure is. Healthiest food on earth," said Washoe, and started to cough.

"You've got to remember this boy doesn't work with a pick and shovel," said Craig. "He obviously hasn't got your consti-tution, MacQueen. If you keep feeding him this stuff, he'll die, and that's no exaggeration."

"Man's got to eat something," murmured Washoe, wiping his hands on his apron.

"Not this one," said Craig. "I don't want him fed another bite of food. It's worse than just his insides clogged up. The bowel has undoubtedly telescoped, the way it's swelled out there. It's too far advanced for anything but an operation."

"No, you don't!" MacQueen's voice fairly shook the room. "Nobody's butchering my kid. My father died of that. He didn't need no operation in the first place. He'd be alive and kicking today if that damn' sawbones hadn't cut him up."

"That was twenty years ago, Dad," said Garnet. "Medicine has advanced just as fast as mining since then. You've got to let Doctor Craig do what's necessary."

"No Craig's touching my boy," said Jada MacQueen.

"What have you got against me, MacQueen?" Craig wondered.

"Now he's asking me," MacQueen told the room.

"Yes," Craig said, "I am."

MacQueen stared at him, the tension of his bitterly restrained anger pinching his eyes in till they were barely visible behind the squinted lids. "Why did you come back here, Craig?"

"To doctor you people," said Craig.

"I'll bet," said MacQueen. "I'd just put my bottom dollar on that."

"Maybe you know some other reason," said Craig in an anger of his own now.

"He's asking me again," said MacQueen. "Hear that, Cousin Jack? He's asking me again."

"I heard," said Cousin Jack.

"I didn't come here to argue with a stubborn, old fool who's prejudiced against all medicine because one man made a mistake twenty years ago," said Craig sharply, irritated beyond restraint. "You must have seen a thousand cave-ins, yet you still go on digging those holes in the ground for gold. Why can't you give medicine the same chance? How about some hot water and clean linen, Garnet? And I'll need a glass for the chloroform."

"Chloroform?" MacQueen's husky, whispered tone was startling after all the shouting. He stared at Craig with that blank, glittering light in his eyes. "Get out, Craig," he said, and started walking toward the doctor. "Get out of here."

The shot drowned all sound. It seemed to fill the room, shaking the very walls with the immensity of its sound. MacQueen stopped half way to Craig, staring at the white piece of wood that had been chipped from the ceiling by the bullet to fall at his feet.

"Next time," said Garnet in a choked, trembling voice, with

the gun pointed at him, "next time, it'll come out of you. I mean it, Dad. Get back."

The prominent thing then was their breathing — a half dozen varieties of sound as MacQueen stared at his daughter: the guttural susurration of his own breath, the shallow, dimly painful breathing of Washoe, the lighter, moaning noise emanating from the boy as he tossed deliriously on the bed. Then it was the acrid scrape of MacQueen's boots, as he stepped backward, till he came against the wall, his eyes still on Garnet. Her mouth was working faintly, and her hands gripped the over-and-under so tightly they were trembling.

"Washoe," said Craig, "I think you'd better get the things I need. A big drinking glass. Keep a gallon of water at a boil. As much clean linen as you can find in the house."

Washoe took a look at MacQueen, then scuttled around Garnet for the kitchen. Craig stripped off his coat and rolled up his sleeves. Then he rigged a line to hang the two bull's eye lanterns in the room above the bed for overhead light. He spread his clean handkerchief on the bedside table, opening his bag to place his scalpel and tenaculum and other tools across it. He was aware that MacQueen's eyes had dropped on the glittering array. Craig studied the line of instruments himself, with the harried sense of having forgotten something. He knew a wish that he had the artery clamps he'd sent East for, instead of that tenaculum, but they had not arrived yet, and that did not seem to be what was bothering him anyway. He could not bring it to mind, and some sullen scrape of boots across the room made him realize what a mistake it would be to let them see hesitation now. He got out his bottle of carbolic solution and began swabbing the boy's stomach.

"What's that?" MacQueen's voice held surly suspicion.

"Carbolic acid," Craig told him.

"Acid!"

34

"It won't hurt him," muttered Craig impatiently. "It's only a five percent solution. We've got to sterilize things some way. They spray the whole room with it now at some hospitals."

"Nobody's putting acid on my boy."

"He's doing it," snapped Garnet. "Shut up."

After swabbing Duncan, Craig began sterilizing his instruments, one by one. Each action brought him nearer to the moment of incision. He found an awesome, suffocating tension mounting within himself, utterly different from the tension he had been working under up to now, a burgeoning compound of doubt and apprehension and indecision that was gaining dangerous strength. And then the thought, a smoky fragment at first, worming its insidious path into his mind, to take on the palpable, echoing repetition of a drumbeat. *Your first major surgery, your first major surgery, your first major. . . .* It brought a keen, thin sickness, way down in his insides, the way a man felt just before a fight. He felt the clammy prickle of sweat break out on his forehead, and barely blocked his impulse to reach up and wipe it off. He could not let MacQueen see this doubt in him. It wasn't his first major operation, really. He had performed them under the supervision of the house surgeons back at Massachusetts General. *Yes, under supervision.*

He turned sharply toward the boy, trying to blot these thoughts from his mind. He stuffed cotton into the bottom of the glass and saturated it with chloroform. He heard MacQueen's jerky, scraping movement as he pressed the upended glass over Duncan's face.

"Doc . . . ," said MacQueen, in a guttural, helpless way.

Craig did not turn toward him. He saw the boy's breathing deepen, gain greater regularity. He lifted the scalpel from the handkerchief. The muscles about his ribs seemed to contract till he could not breathe. This was the moment.

He turned his head in toward the wall so they could not see

his face and closed his eyes, trying to bring all the force of his mind to bear against this insidious doubt. Then he swung back, opening his eyes, and began.

It was a wearying, cramped position, bending over the bed that way. His awareness of the rest of the room faded. His consciousness seemed to become a funnel, directed down to his hands. Time lost significance. Spatial relations became blurred. His whole awareness was in that bright-edged focus of attention on the movements of his hands — movements practiced at the gleaming metal operating tables at the hospital till they became habitual. And, somehow, the bed seemed to become that table. Present and past mingled. And the force moving Craig's hands ceased to be habit. It was words. Dry and passionless words, as clear and concise as the cut of a scalpel. That must be Walsh. Was he house surgeon this year?

Slower, Doctor. You're almost. . . . You're going to have hemorrhage unless you tie that vein. Tenaculum, nurse. Not too far above where you've sewed, Doctor. Catgut, nurse. . . .

Automatically Craig held his left hand out, waiting for the catgut. Then, with a small shock of surprise, he realized there was no nurse, no Walsh, only himself in this fetid, log room, with those men silhouetted against the fading afternoon light in the window, watching in strained attention.

Holding up the severed vein with his tenaculum, he turned to the table for the catgut. And realized, in that instant, what he had forgotten to put out. He reached into his bag but could not feel the box of catgut. Sweat began forming its clammy trail down his neck. He tipped over the bag, shaking out its remaining contents. The box was not there. With a small nausea deep in his loins he remembered taking the box out this morning to check it. He tried to keep his voice level.

"Garnet, I've forgotten my ligatures. I'll need something to tie these veins up with. Some silk thread?"

36

There was a moment of silence, then Garnet's voice broke against it, holding a high, sharp edge of sustained tension. "Washoe, my sewing kit's in the living room. The red spool is silk. Hurry."

Washoe's muted, coughing passage about the other room seemed to fill eternities. Finally he was back with the thread. Craig washed a length of it in the carbolic acid and began to ligate. With the limited, unsatisfactory scope of the tenaculum, he had not been able to prevent bleeding completely. It stained the sheet and blankets, lifting a dark, sticky scent against the smells of sweat and carbolic acid filling the room. Craig had not realized how keyed up he was till a lengthening afternoon shadow touched his arm, and he jumped sharply. MacQueen made a small, mewing sound deep in his throat.

Craig felt the reassuring warmth of a hand on his arm, and turned part way to meet a cool rag, wiping the sweat from his forehead. He had not even heard Garnet ask Washoe for this, but she was holding the gun in one hand as she swabbed at Craig's face with the other. He tried to put his thanks in his eyes. She looked down once at Duncan. Then she turned back, biting her ripe underlip.

It was another space of time without measure or relation. Darkness filled the frames of the windows, creeping in to form musty patches in the farthest corners of the room. The lanterns threw Craig's shadow in black distortion across the bed, to sway at his slightest movement, touching the boy's face with its somber portent.

Craig's eyes began to ache. The pain of tension spread to his hands, and his fingers started to draw up with it. Sweat dripped into his eyes, blinding him, and it was too close to the end to turn for Garnet's cloth again. Craig tried to squint the salty, blinding tears of it away. They dribbled down into his mouth, with their sharp, briny taste. They dripped off his chin onto the blanket. His back ached so much he did not think he could maintain this position another instant.

Then it was through, the suturing and bandaging and everything, and he pulled the blanket up over Duncan, straightening and stepping back. Nobody moved. He began to tremble. Nausea formed a cottony gag deep in his throat. He thought he was going to vomit.

"All right," he said. "That's it."

Garnet slumped onto the bed with a dry, wracked sob, the rifle slipping heedlessly to the floor. MacQueen shook the floor with the passage of his weight, coming over without a word to stare down at Duncan. The man's grizzled, reddish hair was so damp with sweat that most of the curl had left it. He cocked his head to hear the boy's steady, even breathing, and then turned to look at Craig. For a moment he seemed about to speak. Then he shook his head confusedly, and turned back toward Duncan. Craig drew in a heavy, exhausted breath, and started repacking his bag. By the time he was finished, Garnet had recovered herself.

"You'll have something to eat?"

"I'd better not," he murmured. "I won't get back to town before midnight as it is. I'll leave written instructions for Duncan's care. You can see how quiet he is now. If everything goes all right, that's the way he should stay. If he gets overly restless, or seems more feverish, get in touch with me. Otherwise, there's not much I can do for the present. Above all, I don't want you to feed him *anything*. I can't emphasize that strongly enough. If you get more food down there, it will clog up again and probably burst the bowel. That would kill him."

"We'll take care of him," said MacQueen sullenly.

Garnet got a heavy, wine-colored shawl and followed Craig out to the mountain wagon. MacQueen watched them from the front door. Craig helped the woman up to the seat, but, as he was about to follow, MacQueen's voice caused him to turn back. There was some awesome portent to the gigantic silhouette the man made in the saffron rectangle of the doorway.

"If that boy dies, Craig," he said, "I'll be down to town looking for you. Count on that."

Chapter Three

Coffin Gap did not recognize the difference between night and day. When Garnet and Craig returned, a little after midnight, there was as much traffic sucking through the spring mud along Cutbank Street as there had been when they left that morning. Many stores were still open, and the batwing doors of the saloons kept up a steady creaking chorus to the passage of men.

There were few miners in evidence. Since most of the lode mining had pinched out, MacQueen was the only big operator left in the area, and the feeling against him made it dangerous for his men to come down here. So it was freighting and cattle, with the groaning, high-sided Murphy wagons filling the streets at all hours, and hairy, muddy little cow ponies standing hipshot before every hitch rack. Garnet pulled up before the Blackhorn Hotel where Craig was staying, and he climbed down, turning to her.

"You aren't going back tonight?"

She glanced over her shoulder, and he saw her eyes focus on the small crown branded into the hip of one of the horses at a near tie rack. "I'll stay at Brockhalter's store. It's only a couple of miles out of town. He's an ex-miner, and his wife is a cousin of mine. I think it would be better." She stopped, and they gazed at each other in silence. He felt the necessity of saying something, he did not know what. She must have acted under the same impulse, reaching forward to lay a hand over his. "Your father would have been proud of you, Alan," she said in a low, throaty voice. Then, as if in some embarrassment, she turned to take up the reins and call to the team.

As he turned toward the hotel, he found a restlessness stirring him. He was tired clear into his bones, but he was jumpy and nervous, too, in reaction to the grueling day, and he did not feel like going to bed. On the sidewalk his glance was caught by the lights of the Nebuchadnezzar, half a block eastward along Cutbank, on the other side of the street.

The illumination seeping over its batwing doors fell across the man at the curbing. By the expansive way he stood with his legs wide apart, thumbs in the armholes of his gaudy, bed-of-flowers waistcoat, head tilted back to point his cigar skyward, Craig recognized Gabriel Irish. It was the way the man would savor the night. Feeling suddenly a deep craving for his amiable company, after all the sullen hostility at Mac-Queen's, Craig turned down the street.

Irish had been one of Craig's closest friends here, starting in as a bartender in one of the rot-gut saloons farther down Cutbank about the same time Alan's father had begun his Scissors with a quarter-section homestead. He was a man in his late forties, his lustrous brown hair just tinged these last years with gray at the temples and down the heavy sideburns. The ruddy glow of his smooth, unmarred face smacked more of the vine than the sun. Seeing that it was Craig approaching, he let out a hearty chuckle of greeting.

"How's the MacQueen boy, Doctor?"

"My first major, Gabriel," said Craig. "I think every fried potato from here to Butte had been jammed up in his intestines."

"A success, I take it," grinned the man. "How about a drink after your ordeal?"

"You know I'm not much of a drinking man."

"Neither was Bacchus, and they made a god of him." Irish smiled. "Come in and be a god."

Craig could not help reacting to the infectious, urbane humor of the man and felt his smile spread his lips slowly, rising from the tired, sober depths of him till his teeth made

41

a white gleam against the light.

"I'll come in on one condition," Craig told him.

"Name it."

"I've been wondering, ever since I came back, why you called this the Nebuchadnezzar."

"A Nebuchadnezzar," said Irish expansively, "is a bottle for holding champagne. It's the biggest they have and holds twenty quarts. Just consider that, when you walk through these doors."

With a sly twinkle in his eyes, Irish bowed Craig in. The Nebuchadnezzar had once been a barn, and the walls of the immense, single chamber that constituted the whole saloon were hung with great, ballooning squares of wine-colored satin and gaudy chintz that gave it an opulent, Oriental aura. There were the larger gambling tables taking up one side, where a man could buck the tiger or bet on the double 0, and the round short-card tables toward the rear. The bar was of ruddy Philippine mahogany covered with stacks of cut glass that formed winking, glittering prisms of reflected light. All of Irish's men were gentlemen, and Craig saw Gentleman George start to come down toward them from behind the bar. Irish waved him away and moved around the end of the bar himself, slipping a cotton towel from beneath for an apron. This end was comparatively empty of men, and Irish had chosen a spot that would give them some privacy. He rubbed his hands together and asked Craig what it would be.

"Rye, I suppose," Craig answered.

The man snorted disgustedly. "You aren't in any of those forty-rod houses down the street. Let me fix you something befitting the occasion. A tuesseto, shall we say. It won't lift you up like this" — he jerked his thumb viciously into the air — "but it will lift you up like this." He spread both hands out, palms up, and raised them gently, delicately, as if wafting a

42

cloud. "See? Light. Airy. A jolly, carefree bit of pink fuzz blown by the gentlest of bacchanalian zephyrs."

He mixed the drink, setting it before Craig with a flourish. Craig lifted the glass up, deliberately catering to the connoisseur in Irish by passing it under his nose before taking a sip. After the taste he drew the tip of his tongue across his lips and inclined his head appreciatively. This brought a raffish chuckle from Irish.

"I thought you'd like it. Coleridge said that some men are like musical glasses. To produce their finest tones, you must keep them wet."

As the man spoke, Craig's eyes happened to pick up the faces in the back-bar mirror. He surprised half a dozen men, farther down the bar, watching him covertly. He turned his head casually to see the same furtive attention centered on him from men within the crowds about the tables. When he turned back, he saw that Irish was aware of his discovery. The jaunty humor left the man's face.

"Maybe you know something besides quotations," Craig told him.

Irish took up the bar towel and began scrubbing the mahogany thoughtfully. "You surprised a lot of people here in town when you went up on the mountain, Alan."

Craig realized now that the man had brought him in for more reasons than the drink and asked: "Where do you stand, Gabriel?"

"If either MacQueen or the valley men had an ounce of sense in them, they could have worked out something that settled this thing," said Irish, with more heat than Craig was accustomed to in him.

"You're neutral, then?"

"It's easier for a saloon keeper to sit the fence than it will be for a doctor," said Irish.

"I'm glad someone's on it beside me, anyway," smiled Craig ruefully.

Irish met his eyes. "You must have sympathies more in one direction than the other, though, Alan, being the son of Bob Craig."

"Because he was a cattleman?"

"Well" — Irish began wiping the bar again in that vague embarrassment — "that and. . . ."

"That and what?" asked Craig. "I've had it brought to my attention more than once now, Gabriel. Something more than just the fact that Bob Craig was a cattleman, and his son should favor the cattle interests."

Craig thought he saw surprise in the man's sharply raised eyes, before something else replaced it: a sudden shrewd speculation, foreign to Irish.

"You're joking, Alan."

"No," Craig said. "I'd like to know, Irish."

The man frowned at him. "I wouldn't believe that from anybody else."

"Can you believe it from me?"

The man took a heavy breath and went back to polishing the bar, abstractedly, as if bringing thoughts to focus. "How long after your dad was killed did you leave, Alan?" he asked.

"A couple of weeks. I sold most of our saddle stock to Nassaur, and a Laramie concern bought the land and cattle."

"And at that time you didn't know how your father's death came about?"

"He was shot out on the range."

Irish pursed his lips. "I never meant to tell you this, Alan, but some folks were a little disappointed in you when you left. They thought Bob Craig's death should be revenged."

"How?" asked Craig. "There were so many high-line riders down off the Missions in those days, it would have taken me a lifetime to uncover who did it. You know the trouble we were having with rustling then, Gabriel. I tried to get a line on it, but it was hopeless. I guess I didn't have it in me to dedicate my life to revenge." He stopped, staring at Irish, and it came out in a reluctant, attenuated way. "You?"

"Now, now," said Irish, swinging his lustrous head from side to side. "You know I wasn't disappointed in you, Alan. I tried to get a line on who killed Bob at that time myself, and, as you say, it was hopeless. Just that talk."

"What talk?"

The man peered at him from beneath his brows. "You really don't know, do you?"

"I told you."

Irish stopped polishing, leaned forward on his elbows to bring his face closer to Craig's across the bar. "I guess the talk must have started after you left. Did Jada MacQueen ever enter your mind?"

Craig started to frown with a lack of understanding. Then he did understand. He felt angry irritation tighten his face. That flattened to a bleakness.

"Why should it? MacQueen?" He frowned again. "This business hadn't started then. Jada was still *digging* his gold out at that time."

"Your outfit watered out of Bucket Creek, didn't it? That was the first creek bed MacQueen's hydraulicking started filling up."

"But there hadn't been any trouble over it, Gabriel."

"Do you know the exact date MacQueen started hydraulicking?"

Craig started to answer that heatedly, then clamped his lips shut as the idea gained its insidious hold on him. "No," he said almost defiantly, "I don't."

"MacQueen's bookkeeper used to get drunk in here once

in a while," Irish told him. "He talked a lot when he did, and I'm never one to plug my ears. He told me MacQueen started his first hydraulic operations on August the seventh, Eighteen Seventy-Four. That was about ten days before your father was killed, wasn't it?"

Craig was staring beyond Irish now with an intense frown on his face, unwilling to accept the implications of this, trying to fit it together right, to remember whether his father had said anything about a clash with MacQueen before his death. He couldn't. It just wasn't there. But he could remember what MacQueen had said this very evening. *A Craig's touching my boy.* With special emphasis on the name. *Craig!* Not doctor. *Craig!*

He shook his head from side to side with the ugliness of it. "You mean MacQueen . . . ?"

"That's the general idea," said Irish. "Whether MacQueen actually was responsible for your father's death, or just heard the talk accusing him of it, isn't it logical for him to assume that you've come back wanting revenge?" Irish reached out to grab Craig's arm as the doctor started whirling away. "Where are you going?"

"To get my buckboard and go back up to MacQueen's. I've got to clear this up right now."

"Take it easy, Alan. If MacQueen's got that idea set in his mind, a ton of his Giant Powder wouldn't blast it loose. You know what a stubborn, old fool he is. Let your actions speak. You've gone up to tend his boy now. If he pulls through, that will help a lot. You've got other things to watch besides Mac-Queen."

Some darkening inflection of the man's voice caused Craig to turn back. "What's that?"

Irish allowed his hand to slide off, and started wiping the bar again. "Bowie French. He was in town looking for you this evening, Alan, and he was all alone."

The only light when Craig left the Nebuchadnezzar was the reflection of the moon, gleaming feebly from the muddy ruts of the street. There were still some saloons open farther down toward Territory Road, and a train of freight wagons moving eastward toward the Kootenai, but the noise of that slipped behind Craig as he crossed Second Street, moving out of the saloon district. There were more business buildings up here, their darkened walls throwing up muffled echoes to the sodden clatter of his boots along the plank walks still damp from rain. Or was it the walls echoing him?

He halted a moment in the black shadow of a wooden overhang fronting the harness shop. No answering sound filled the silence his pause left.

I'm tired, he told himself, *a man's always jumpy when he's tired.* He started walking again when he caught a furtive movement at the corner, across Cutbank. This time he blocked his desire to halt, going on down the walk in deliberate, clattering steps. He was almost to his hotel when the spotted hound dog scuttled from the shadows over there.

He could not deny the relief in the way his breath left him. He moved on to the hotel, no longer trying to evade the thought that kept nagging at him. *Bowie French? All right, Bowie French. Bowie wanted to see him, that was all.* Yet he found himself glancing swiftly, almost furtively, at the single horse standing before a hitch rack across the street. It did not bear the Coronet brand.

Trying to shrug off his apprehension, he pushed through the clouded, dirty glass doors of the Blackhorn. The man nodding behind the desk came up in his chair with a startled jerk, blinking stupidly. He was a sloppy, kettle-bellied man with nothing more than a rawhide vest covering the grimy upper

47

portion of his long, woolen underwear. Greasy, shaven creases ridged the back of his neck, just below the bullet dome of his perfectly bald head, and the doughy flesh of his cheeks was mottled with the purpling pattern of broken veins.

"You working all the time, Marcus?" Craig asked him.

Bill Marcus picked a ragged plug of tobacco off the desk and took a vicious bite out of it. "Night man took sick again, damn him! Wish you'd either kill him or cure him."

"I'll have a look," Craig murmured. "Any mail for me? I'm expecting some artery clamps from the East."

"Nothing along that line," growled the manager. "Man waiting for you in the lobby, though."

Craig halted with yet one step to go to the desk, his hand already lifting to get his key. For an instant he felt a strange, winded emptiness at the pit of his stomach. Then he dropped his hand. His smile was a definite effort.

"Thanks, Marcus," he said. "You can go back to sleep now."

Through the wide double doors leading into the main part of the lobby he could see the potted palms lining the long front window in their wilted attempt at splendor, the faded, stained rug with its nap worn through in a semicircle before the sagging leather couch and armchairs. The man was not in sight from here, and, as Craig passed toward the doors, he caught the reflection of his own face in a battered Adamesque mirror, hanging on this side of the portal. There was something gray about it. The lines about his mouth had a pinched, whitened look that seemed more than weariness. *Well, why not?* It would be different than the meeting he had been envisioning between Bowie and himself. That business with Evan Fox and Ingo Hubbard couldn't help changing things. It would be a lot different.

Then he was through the door and could see the only man in the room, and it was not Bowie French. He was a square,

48

ugly little man, with a Neanderthal face, starkly primitive in its furrowed, receding brow and simian jaw. His sack suit was shoddy and stained, his flat-heeled boots caked with the singular reddish clay of Cheyenne Flats.

"You the new doc?" he asked and went on without waiting for Craig to speak, making violent gestures with his hands to illustrate almost every word. "I'm Asa Gardener. Been waiting since seven, Doc. My wife's sick out on the Flats. Feverish off and on for about a week. Try to get her in bed and she won't. Now her leg's swole up and big red spots all over her body."

"Round spots, about the size of my hand, go away when you press them?" said Craig.

"Yes." The man's hands stopped moving in surprise. "How'd you know? That's it exactly. Never saw the like."

"You got a rig?" Craig asked.

"No. Hopped a ride on a freight wagon."

"Let's get my buckboard from the stable," Craig told him.

Field's Livery stood on the corner of Fifth and Cutbank, an immense, hip-roofed barn set back from the street, with old harness and wagon rigs littering the broad, hoof-beaten compound in front. Harry Fields came down after Craig had beaten his knuckles raw on the front doors. He was a twisted, rheumatic little old man, with gray hair roached like a mule's mane and eyes as young and black as an Indian girl's. Grumbling sleepily, he brought out the white mare first, hitching her up to the buckboard parked on the compound. Then he got the black mare, running a hand affectionately down the heavy-muscled chest as he backed her into the double tree.

"You got a wonderful team here, Doc," he said. "It's hard to believe they're the same animals your dad prized so high."

"They do look young, don't they?" Craig agreed. "They were the one thing of the Scissors I couldn't sell, Harry. I had them shipped back East and used them all during my training."

49

Fields watched Craig's eyes as they ran over the fine, clean lines of the two mares. "I guess you love them as much as your pa did," chuckled the stableman.

"If they were both one woman, I'd marry her," smiled Craig.

Fields snorted. "Why bring women into it?"

They left the old man standing bowlegged in his door, lighting their way out of the compound with his bull's eye. The air was still damp from recent rain, and it put vinegar in Pepper and Salt as they broke into a trot down Cutbank, their hoofs forming a steady slopping sound against the muddy street. They passed the Blackhorn, and the darkened Nebuchadnezzar. They passed the junction of Territory Road and Cutbank Street. About a hundred yards beyond this intersection Asa Gardener turned nervously in the seat to look behind. Some lifting motion of his body caused Craig to cast a glance over his shoulder in the same direction. A rider had come out of Territory Road to halt his horse on Cutbank. He sat there, watching them, until Craig could no longer see him.

Gardener turned his face back to the front, interlacing his fingers in a tense, nervous gesture. "Now I wonder what that could mean?" he muttered.

"You in trouble?" Craig asked.

Gardener glanced at him. "Heard you went up the mountain to fix MacQueen's boy today, Doc. Take a good look at me and see what you are in for. When I first come up from Cheyenne three years ago, I was a successful man. Lived in a big house down on Seventh Street, had a dozen teams as pretty as yours. Had most of the worthwhile lumber contracts tied up around here. Then I made the mistake of going up on the mountain, too. MacQueen offered me a contract to supply him with all the lumber he'd need for operations. That meant a big chunk of money. He's always needing to build new flumes and shore up those adits. I thought I was big enough to buck the

50

beef interests and took the contract. Those cattlemen broke me in three months. Haven't been able to get off my knees since."

Craig stared at the man. Asa Gardener was looking straight ahead, and he did not say another word till they reached his place.

Cheyenne Flats was no more than a mudbank formed by the high clay bluffs that ran from the Cutbank Bridge northward along the edge of the Kootenai River. It was made up of every type of building, skin teepees of the degenerate ration Indians, old Army tents, log cabins abandoned by earlier trappers. Craig found Gardener's wife in a sod hut dug out of a claybank and roofed over with tarpaper and willows. A putrid pile of rags sufficed for the blankets covering the children in the front room. Mrs. Gardener lay on a buffalo robe thrown over willow boughs in the back chamber.

Craig went down on his knees in the mud of the floor, oblivious now to the appalling squalor as he examined the woman. Her head was tilted back to throw her hair like the stringy, lifeless tendrils of a mop down over the end of the buffalo robe. Her eyes were fixed on his face in a listless, uncaring way, and her breathing was shallow and painful. Craig knew what it was already, but he made a patient, thorough examination. When he was finished, he got to his feet again, dank clay dripping off his trousers.

"Your wife has typhoid fever, Gardener. The first thing you've got to do is get her out of here."

"Where to, Doc? I ain't got no relatives in a thousand miles."

"I don't mean that. A clean place. What's your water supply here?"

"The river."

Craig shook his head dismally, turning as was his habit, to pace across the room, halting himself within a step as he saw how small it was. He made an angry, impatient gesture with

51

one hand. "You couldn't boil that water ten times over and have it fit to drink. What about your privy vaults here? I suppose they're all open."

"Out behind the house. We just use a hole and cover it up."

Craig raised his face to the ceiling, closing his eyes. "And your sewage, your garbage? I suppose you just dump it all in the river."

"What don't go out in the woods. Everybody does that way."

"Look at the flies in this room. Don't you screen any opening off?"

"We ain't got glass, much less screen," said Gardener. "You're down in the Flats now, Doc."

"It isn't much better in town," said Craig. "You've still got to get her out of here, Gardener, if you don't want to cause an epidemic. If you can't find a place, I'll make some arrangements in town. There must be some place we can isolate these cases. Can you read?"

"Only my name and Abe Lincoln's."

Craig took a deep breath. "Then I'll have to tell you. Clean her up first, understand? Boil all the water you wash her in. Don't give her any more to drink. Get clean blankets from somewhere . . . a neighbor . . . surely you can manage that? Put a cloth in this open window. Keep that front door closed. Free the place of flies somehow. I'll bring you some carbolic acid to dump in your privy vaults tomorrow. The only thing I want her to drink is milk. If she loses it pure, mix some lime water with it."

"Where'll I get that, Doc?"

"Milk? With all the cattle in this valley?"

"They're only interested in beef," said Gardener, genuinely alarmed now. "I bet you couldn't find one cattleman in a million who could milk one of his cows. I sure couldn't!"

"Then get some canned milk. I'll find that in town, too.

Meantime, feed her some barley water or beef tea." The bucolic expression on the man's face, staring at him, comprehending none of this, brought an exasperated snort from Craig. He drew a weary breath. "Here, we'll start all over again. Help me undress her. We'll wash her together."

.

Chapter Four

Dawn was silhouetting the Cabinets to the southwest before Craig got off the Flats, leaving with a vague, harrying sense of frustration. Gardener was deeply worried about his wife, sincere in his desire to improve her condition. But his appalling ignorance of the most fundamental necessities in cleanliness and medical care had blocked Craig at every turn, until the doctor found himself in unreasoning anger at the man. He drove through the shanties and tents, confident that there would be no screening of any sort on the doors or windows, that just as many flies would fill the room, and that the carbolic acid would not be put in the sewage and privy vaults unless he himself saw to it.

Each house in the Flats was no better, however, as he drove down the winding, littered path leading to Cutbank Street. A morning wind stirred piles of refuse against the rotting log walls of a building, fluttered the paper labels on tin cans littering the ground, wafted the reek of garbage and open cesspools to Craig. It filled him with a deep, angry impulse to see the filth swept away, and he entered town in this mood. He stabled his team, shaved and washed in his hotel room before going down for breakfast. He thought of getting a little shut-eye before noon, but sleep would not come, and he knew why. Driven by it, he dressed and went into the street.

There was no city hall, Craig found out. The mayor and councilmen kept part-time offices in a frame building on the corner of Cutbank and First. Here, an indifferent janitor told the doctor he could find Mayor Donovan at his butcher shop on Cutbank and Third. There were four butchers behind the counter, but Donovan seemed to do none of the work himself, merely standing around in a gaudy, padded marseilles waist-coat, emphasizing his conversation with a group of idlers at the chopping block by emphatic stabbing motions with his fat cigar. Most of his prosperity seemed to have gone to his stomach and jowls, and he greeted Craig with the professional heartiness of a man who felt his station a little too keenly. He gave Craig's desire to speak to him alone great importance, assuring the idlers he would be back soon, and then led Craig to the rear of the shop with a glad hand on the doctor's back.

Craig did not waste any time, telling the mayor what he had seen down in Cheyenne Flats. Donovan agreed with him, saying that they meant to clean it up as soon as they could get around to it.

"You'll have to do it now, if you don't want an epidemic of major proportions," Craig told him. "One case of typhoid in a place like that means others."

"What do you want, Doctor?" frowned the mayor, gnawing at his cold cigar.

"Some kind of hospital, first of all, where we can isolate these cases. Any kind of decent building with adequate sewage and screening and a few practical nurses. A town this size should have had that long ago."

"You forget, buildings are at a premium," the man muttered.

"They don't seem to be for saloons or gambling halls," Craig told him. "That building Matt Tracy moved his Four Aces into last week is big enough for two hospitals. You can find a building if you get the town behind it, Mayor."

The man occupied himself lighting his cigar, dropping the match when it was going to grind it carefully in the sawdust with his hobnailed heel. "It's harder than just going out and getting a building, Craig. It's a big problem."

"A typhoid epidemic is a big problem, too," said Craig. "It won't stop with Cheyenne Flats, Donovan. The best part of

55

your town isn't in much better condition than those shanties out there when it comes to sewage and screening and water supply."

"You can blame MacQueen for that," said Donovan. "If we had decent water. . . ."

Craig hung onto his patience with great care. "I'll grant you the water is the main problem. But polluted water isn't the only carrier. Typhoid breeds in those open sewers, Donovan. The flies pick it up and bring it right back into an unscreened house. Ninety-five percent of your buildings in Coffin Gap aren't screened."

"And never have been," said Donovan. "Do you know what you're asking, Doctor? Half the people here don't know what screens are. We'd have to ship them in from the East. Do you have any idea what a sewage system for this whole town would cost? Things like that just can't be done overnight. We're working on it."

"You've gotten a lot done," said Craig acidly. "The town's been here for over nine years, and you still haven't got an inside toilet to your name. Flies swarming into every building along Cutbank. Look at that counter." He swept a hand toward the quarters of beef hung behind the butchers, covered with flies. "Every one of these insects is a potential carrier. How many people do you sell meat to every day? If there's an epidemic, you'll be one of the most direct causes, Donovan."

"Look here, Craig," said the man in a loud, righteous voice, poking the cigar at him so hard it went out again, "I've been selling my meat like this for years and never had a complaint before. . . ."

"You've had typhoid before, haven't you? Almost every year . . . ?" Craig halted himself with great effort, seeing the anger reddening the man's face. "There's no point in arguing like this, Mayor. Let's get back to the hospital. I've already got a case of typhoid out in the Flats. If we don't isolate her and start cleaning things up out there, the epidemic will be on its way. Isn't there some kind of building in town we can fix up for a place to put them till we get a regular hospital?"

Pouting, Donovan fished another match from his pocket, sweeping it across the back of one leg. "Council meets this Friday. I'll talk to them about it."

"That will be too late."

"Let it be, then," shouted the mayor, throwing the match disgustedly to the floor as it went out. "I can't buy you a nice, shiny new hospital with a side of beef, Craig. Those things take time. Bonds to pass, money to raise, even if the council does approve it. If you think it's so easy to do, go out and build it yourself!"

Craig was in no mood to placate the man. He did not think it could be done anyway. He saw a derisive smile on the face of one of the idlers — as he wheeled to walk past the chopping block — and had a bitter desire to smash it off with his fist. He spent the rest of the morning looking for the councilmen. Two of them were out on spring roundup, a third would not see him, though Craig knew the man was home. The other two were evasive to the point of angering the doctor again, and he only succeeded in antagonizing them, too. Realizing he could get no satisfaction this way, he began canvassing the private homes for a place to put Mrs. Gardener. When they heard what she had, they did not try to hide their fear of it, and nothing he could offer would make them take her in. Then he went to the hotels. It was the same story there. Even his own hotel would not rent her a room. In an exhausted rage he turned his buckboard out toward the Flats about three that afternoon.

One of the children was sitting half dressed on the floor in the front room of the shack, piling mud over her bare legs. Gardener was crouched over his wife's bed, murmuring to her, a balding, pitiable figure in his distress. There were no screens up, and the flies still swarmed over the room. With all the exhausting frustration of the day behind him, Craig was unable to contain himself.

"I thought I told you to put cloth over those windows and clean this place out," he told the man sharply. "It stinks like a pigsty!"

Gardener turned a hurt, twisted face up to him, and his eyes looked like those of a kicked dog. "I tried, Doc, but Sarah started moaning it was too hot in here all closed up. I couldn't see her suffering that way."

"Don't you understand, Gardener, those flies are the carriers? They take it from your house all over the. . . ." Craig stopped, shaking his head heavily. "Never mind. I'm too tired to try and beat it into your head. Help me get her in the wagon. We're taking her to town."

The man brightened. "You got a place?"

"Yes," said Craig grimly, "I got a place."

The children had to go also, for there was no one to watch them, and, with the whole family loaded into his buckboard, Craig drove back to town, right down the middle of Cutbank and up to the Blackhorn Hotel. A crowd began gathering as he and Asa Gardener lifted Sarah out of the wagon and carried her in through the front door of the hotel. Bill Marcus stared at them in angry surprise from behind the desk. When he rose, the movement drew an attenuated belch from him. He moved heavily around into the entrance hall, blocking their way with his immense kettle belly.

"I told you we wouldn't rent any rooms to that lady, Craig."

"I'm taking her to my room, Marcus," Craig told him.

"I'll have the law on you."

"You won't have any grounds for it," Craig answered. "She's the only one who's going to sleep there. My rent's paid. You won't find any statute in this town's books to get her out. Now, are you going to move aside, or are you going to make trouble?"

The manager stood before them another moment, jaws clamped shut so hard over the bulge of chewing tobacco in one cheek they stretched the flesh like a drumhead. His eyes did not actually move from Craig's face, but for a moment some small shift in the focus of his attention seemed to carry it downward until it reached the shape of Craig's gun beneath his coat. The man's chin lowered into his neck, forming slack, greasy furrows. "I'll have the law on you," he repeated sullenly, backing out of their way.

They carried Sarah Gardener on up to the second floor, and to Craig's room, but barely had her comfortable in bed when a knock shook the door. Gardener straightened up from his wife, glancing in a sharp, apprehensive way at Craig. The doctor moved to open the door and found Marcus there, with Marshal Walter Ashfield. The marshal was a tall man, wearing a pair of faded Army blues with the canary yellow stripe of the cavalry running down the leg. His face held more force than thought, with its heavy, powerful jaws, and his eyes were filled with the keen, instant comprehension of a man used to sizing up a situation in one glance.

"You'll have to get her out, Craig," he said quietly.

"Have you got a warrant?" Craig asked him.

"I don't need one," said the marshal. "I'm here with the owner's permission."

"My room rent's paid till next Saturday," said Craig. "Until then you can't enter my premises without a warrant."

A faint, baffled look lit Ashfield's eyes for a moment. "Don't make trouble, Craig. This woman endangers the whole hotel here . . . the whole town."

"Not so much as if she were out on the Flats," said Craig. "This is one of the few buildings in Coffin Gap with screens.

If Marcus will clean up his sewage, she'll be much more isolated here than out there."

"I'll ask you once more, Craig," said Ashfield. "Don't make me use force."

Craig narrowed his eyes, peering at Ashfield. "Isn't your wife about eight months along now?"

The baffled look returned to Ashfield's eyes. "Yeah, ought to be pretty soon now."

"What will you do to me if I refuse to let you take this woman?"

"Damn you, Doc, don't make it hard for me. . . ."

"Put me in jail, Ashfield? Can I deliver your baby from a cell?"

"Don't let him twist you around, Ashfield," said Marcus angrily.

But Craig saw that he had Ashfield going, and pressed in. "We'll be having a lot of typhoid by the time your baby comes, Ashfield, if the council doesn't do something about a hospital and to clean up this city. Your house isn't in any condition for a nursing mother and her newborn child to live in during an epidemic. I might have to bring them to this hotel. What would you do then? Kick your own wife and baby out onto the streets?"

"Ashfield!" said Marcus sharply.

The marshal turned toward him, shaking his head like a dog out of the water. "He's right, Marcus . . . I . . . I. . . ."

"What's that spot on your neck?" said Craig. Deep, leathery furrows formed in Ashfield's chin as he turned it into his neck, staring downward.

"Where, Doc?"

"There, that rash."

"What rash?"

"Do you know the symptoms of typhoid, Marshal?"

The man turned eyes blank with surprise, and something

else, to Craig. "What are they, Doc?"

Craig shrugged. "If you have any fever, come to my office. Your house isn't fit for anybody with that."

Ashfield grabbed at his arm. "Doc."

"I'm going now," said Craig, meeting his eyes levelly. "You won't do anything about Missus Gardener, will you, Ashfield?"

Without waiting for an answer, he turned and left a miserable, confused officer of the law standing in the open door. Only Gardener followed him, and two doors down Craig halted for him.

"I don't think Ashfield will do anything," he told the man. "If there is trouble, call me at the Nebuchadnezzar. I've got to get some sleep, Asa. Just keep her quiet and don't give her anything but barley water boiled over three or four times. I'll see her as soon as I wake up."

It had begun to rain when he stepped outside. He took his horses to the livery stable and then walked the two blocks to the Nebuchadnezzar. Irish was at the rear by the empty roulette tables, and he came forward hurriedly to greet Craig by the bar.

"You got some kind of sleeping room I can use, Irish? I'm dead."

"You can use my quarters upstairs in the rear," the man grinned. "So you really got her into the Blackhorn?"

Craig could not summon much surprise. "Things pass around fast."

"Everything." The man was still grinning. "I wish you'd quit trying to turn this town upside down in one day. It's hard on my chandeliers. Maybe a little toddy before you drop off?"

"You'll make a drunkard out of me yet, Irish."

"You would refute Emerson?"

"I suppose he had something to say on the subject."

"He thought God made yeast as well as dough, and loved fermentation as dearly as vegetation," answered Irish.

Craig waved his hand in weak defense. "I'm too tired to argue. Just show me the bed."

"A drink first," said Irish. With a swift transition of mood he turned grandiloquently to the shelves. "If you're too tired to argue, you're too tired to sleep. You'll be tossing and turning and getting yourself all tied up in knots unless I give you something to relax you. How about Falerno? Red as an Italian sunset. Juvenal said Sufeja could drink thirty-five gallons of this at a sitting without getting drunk, simply by tickling his throat with a peacock's feather. I even have the feather, if you like."

"Just the bed, Irish, just the bed."

"After your drink," grinned Irish, pouring the wine. "Did you think to bring things to a head by putting Sarah Gardener right in the middle of it?"

"It might frighten a few people into action," shrugged Craig. "I wasn't thinking of the hospital so much, though. She just couldn't stay out on the Flats and live, that's all."

"It won't frighten anyone into action unless the Coronet says so," Irish told him. This brought Craig's head up in surprise. The other man's brows rose to puckish apexes. "Surely you know Donovan is only the errand boy."

"For Coronet?" frowned Craig. "I didn't know Bowie had grown that big."

Irish shrugged. "You'll talk to Donovan all year and never get one screen put up if Bowie has turned thumbs down on it."

"You mean he has?"

"He didn't want you going up to MacQueen, did he?" said Irish. "And you did. Now the wagon's turned around. It strikes me as odd that you haven't seen Bowie French yet."

"I guess you're right. It's about time I did see him."

Chapter Five

Craig woke late the next morning, saw Mrs. Gardener in the hotel, answered a call out on Territory Road, and from there headed for the Coronet. It was an oppressive drive. Threatening thunderheads piled their black tiers behind the Cabinets. A sullen, unseasonable heat filled the basin, permitting only a small, vagrant breeze to stir the tall, foamy plumes of bear grass siding the road. The wagon road to the Coronet turned off Territory Road just before Fisher Bridge. It climbed a leisurely, winding grade into foothills matted with scrub oak. Bucket Creek drained into these from its confluence with the Fisher higher up in the Cabinets, and Craig turned off the Coronet road at the ford, going a mile out of his way to see the Scissors. He was surprised at how much he still thought of it in terms of personal possession and how shocked and angered he felt with sight of its degeneration.

Craig and his father had put up these buildings on the flats at the base of the western slope of the foothills. Silt from Bucket Creek had backed up through the last years to flow across the low ground until it was three or four feet higher than the foundations of the Scissors house, spilling in through sagging, open doorways and obliterating window sills. Craig knew a surge of thoughtless anger at Jada MacQueen which he suppressed with an effort.

The bunkhouse had been built on higher ground behind the main building, and the silt had not yet reached it. There were signs of recent occupancy, fresh droppings in the pack-pole corral and tin cans littering the door stoop with labels not yet curled and browned with age. But no one was here now.

Finally, in a depressed, nostalgic mood, Craig went on.

There were still the broad meadows of buffalo grass and blue root that reminded him of the earlier days here, but, every time he neared a loop of the Fisher or one of its tributaries, the fact was advertised a mile away by the silt piled on the ground, choking off the graze. In some places it was so deep that the road had been cut through it, leaving banks higher than Craig's buckboard. Finally he rose again into the foothills and the Coronet.

He came out of the shielding scrub oak into the compound and almost stopped the wagon in surprise. Having had impressed upon him ever since he returned the extent of the Coronet's holdings and power, he had logically assumed its home pastures would reflect the usual affluence inevitably associated with such a vast ranch. Yet there was only one word for the buildings before him. Squalid.

He pulled in toward the main house, frowning at the dilapidated snake fence running haphazardly down one side of the compound till it collapsed near the road, a hundred yards lying in fallen disrepair. The corrals showed the same lack of care. There were two bunkhouses, merely sodhouses dug out of a hill, one of them shingled with flattened tin cans. The cookhouse was only a tent, blackened with soot and smoke, surrounded by a litter of broken utensils and empty cans and old bones that reminded him of Cheyenne Flats. There were half a dozen men lounging around the corrals and bunkhouses, and three more sitting on the broad, unfinished steps of the main building.

The first one to rise there, at sight of Craig, was Ingo Hubbard. He tucked his great bony hands into his gun belt and leaned carefully back against a splintery support of the porch roof, a sullen, waiting speculation in his milky eyes. The gaunt, dour surface of his face, however, was as darkly expressionless as an Indian's. It brought a dull, small jump of nerves through

64

Craig, filling him with a tightening expectancy. He halted his buckboard near one end of the long porch, recognizing the second of the three men now. It was Timothy Dunnymead who had been working for Henri Nassaur's Cocked Hat when Craig left nine years before.

Dunnymead had an ancient, wizened face, the fuzz of age filling the wrinkles where his scraggly beard didn't grow. The same Absaroka peace pipe, with its stem cut short, was clamped between his few remaining teeth, with its same smell of kinnikinnick reaching Craig in a dim, rank tide as he stepped out of the buckboard and walked toward them. He would always associate the reek of that Indian tobacco with the old man and with that sad, bitter night at the MacBell House so long ago.

You won't find a doctor here, boy. That's one animal we ain't got.

Craig shook the memory away with a savage little movement of his head. Evan Fox was the third man on the porch steps, on his feet now too. Craig halted before him, meeting levelly the patent hostility of his pinched, sour gaze.

"Afternoon, Fox. How's the stomach?"

"My stomach's all right," said Fox in a thin, edged tone. "It doesn't hold things as long as the mind, Craig."

"Hate to see you cherish a grudge, Evan," Craig told him. "Bowie in?"

The man's high, wooden heels made a restless, scraping movement against the hoof-beaten earth before the steps. "He ain't fit to be seen," he answered sullenly.

"Sick?"

"Everybody in the world ain't sick, Doctor," replied Evan sarcastically. "I just don't want to be the one that takes you to Bowie, that's all. Go in, if you want. I don't care."

All the while Timothy Dunnymead had stood there, on the opposite side of the porch from Ingo, drawing deeply on his

65

pipe. Craig glanced at his face, trying to read it, but the old man would give him no satisfaction. As Craig went past Fox and up the steps, Ingo Hubbard rolled his tongue around the inside of his cheeks, as dark and leathery as sun-cured rawhide, and deliberately spat on the top step in front of Craig.

A swift impulse of anger ran through the doctor. It must have shown on his face, for Ingo began to change the weight of his body against the post without actually moving away from it. Dunnymead took his pipe from his mouth in a quick gesture, and Fox's boots scraped again with his wheeling motion to watch this. Craig was surprised at how little effort it took to abort the anger in him, turning it to a mild, indifferent smile.

"Someday, Ingo," he said, "I may make you wipe that up."

The man's milky eyes went blank with a baffled look. Craig moved past before any other reaction could come. He heard the man make some sound behind him, but he did not look back. He opened the door and stepped into the house. The living room ran the length of the house, a fetid, littered den. There must have been a fire at one time, for half of the low, undressed beams frowning down on the room were charred and blackened at the end over the fireplace. There was no facing to cover the rude logs of the outer wall, and chinking from these had piled up unheeded on the floor at the base. Coals glowed sullenly in the great, stone fireplace; the tattered bear rug before this gave off a heavy reek of rot and mold and accumulated filth spilled upon it through the years by whoever had sat in the half dozen wooden-pegged chairs on either side. The silence held a palpable, hostile pressure for Craig, and he closed the front door behind him with a loud clatter to announce his presence.

No answer came from the half-open doors at either end of the main room. He found the thought of Bowie forming a strange, sinister pressure in his mind and tried to blot it out.

66

There should be no apprehension, meeting an old friend like this. It would be so easy to sit down and talk it out with Bowie. He paced the length of the room, glancing covertly through the door at that end. All he could see was a strip of wall as crude and unfinished as the living room and the corner of a filthy, hooked rug.

"Bowie?" he called. "You around? It's Craig."

There was a sibilant stirring from that room. He found a tension tugging his body erect. *This is childish,* he thought. *An old friend like Bowie?* The door opened slowly, until it stood completely ajar. He did not try to hide the violence of his surprise. His voice struck the silence with husky impact.

"Nola?"

She did not speak. She stood in that utter quiescence of body and spirit she had always seemed so capable of, with all the strangely Oriental capacities of her Indian blood. The gloom of the room gave haunting emphasis to the exotic piquancy of her face, with the tawny obliquity of its high cheekbones and narrow, pointed chin, the sense of infinite, ageless depth to her eyes. Some faint movement of her hand caused the dim light to glint across something on her finger. She had never worn jewelry before, and it drew his eye. It was the fourth finger, left hand.

"Not you and Bowie?" he asked, surprised at his own reluctance to voice it.

"Yes, Alan," she said in a calm, fatalistic way. "I thought you didn't mean to come back."

It held tantalizing innuendo, somehow, and he searched her face for the true meaning of it. When he had left for the East, nine years before, she had been sixteen — the daughter of Henri Nassaur, a Frenchman who had been in the fur trade during the 'Fifties and whose fur post in this valley had become the first cattle ranch. Nassaur had married an Absaroka squaw, and, though their daughter was of mixed blood and often called half-breed or *metisse* by some with that mixture of contempt and sly lust they could put into the word when it concerned a woman, she really bore all the aristocratic refinement that was Henri Nassaur's heritage.

Craig had seen much of her during those years, since the Scissors had bordered on Nassaur's Cocked Hat, but what had lain between himself and Nola was a tacit, unspoken thing, as tenuous, as intangible as the forces making up the girl herself. Her attraction was not the bold, vital ripeness of Garnet's beauty. It was something soft, subtle, silken — the purr of a cat, the swift, lost touch of satin passing through the fingers. Craig had left it with a sense of something undeveloped. He found it now, after so many years, filling him with that same groping sensation. Disturbed by it, he took refuge in the prosaic.

"I heard your father died a couple of years after I left, Nola," he said. "I'm sorry."

Some indefinable disappointment shadowed her eyes. Then she nodded, her glance dropping. "I guess I should have written. You thought a lot of Dad, didn't you?"

He felt the stiffness that had descended between them. He sought something to dissipate it, and found nothing. Her eyes, lifting once more to his, had returned to that deep, withdrawn watchfulness.

"If you came to see Bowie, Alan, you'd better come back some other time."

"What's the matter with him, Nola? Evan intimated the same thing. Can I help?"

"He's in one of his moods, that's all."

"One of his moods?"

Her brows raised faintly. "You don't know?"

"No," he said impatiently. "I don't. He never had any moods

68

when I knew him. Is it something recent?"

She turned away in a sharp movement, the line of her shoulders lifting. "I don't know, Alan. I don't think you want to see him now, that's all."

"I've got to. I don't have much spare time, Nola, and it's important."

She turned an oblique glance to him, then she shrugged, and moved through the open door. She crossed that room and stopped before another closed door beyond, knocking softly. There was no answer.

"Bowie," she called softly.

"Go away." The voice was muffled, guttural, to Alan unrecognizable as Bowie's.

"Bowie. Alan's here. Alan Craig."

"Tell him to go away. I don't want to see him. I don't want to see anybody, damn you."

Frowning, Craig stepped to the door behind her. She moved aside, watching him in a fearful, fascinated way. He opened the door. The movement following this came from within, a dim, violent impression of Bowie French across a small, cluttered den of a room, whirling around to grab up a chair by one leg and swinging it back of him to throw. Alan took a step into the room, making himself a perfect target.

"You aren't going to throw that at me, are you, Bowie?" he grinned.

Bowie French glared at him for an instant without moving. Then, with a backward sweep of his arm, he threw the chair into the opposite corner of the room and paced swiftly, viciously to a heavy, leather-seated swivel chair before a small pigeonhole desk, and dropped heavily into it. He stared at the wall before him for a moment, and then threw out his arm in a vicious, sweeping gesture at Nola, without looking toward her.

"Get that tart out of here, by God, before I shoot her."

Craig turned to Nola, an apologetic expression growing in his face. But before he spoke, she stepped back out of the door. Her eyes were fixed on his face in that wide, shining way, like a child or a very old, very wise woman, seeming to hold so much just behind that luminous, expressionless surface, yet showing nothing. Craig seemed to see them even after he had shut the door. Then he turned back and picked up the overturned chair Bowie had thrown down, straddling it, and folding his arms over the top of it. He took a moment to study Bowie, seeking some signs of the man he had known before.

There was animal in Bowie French, candid, bestial, beautiful animal. His hair had a shaggy, leonine look to it, bleached white on top by the sun, corn yellow farther down, the tawny bronze of its original color showing through these other hues in vagrant, coppery streaks. His brows hung in that same leonine shagginess over the restless, incessant movement of eyes the color of hazelnuts. That restlessness characterized the rest of him, a look of intense, driven energy holding the lines of his body tight and hard. He was as tall as Craig, with even less meat in his long legs and narrow shanks. All his weight lay up in his chest and shoulders, building deep, quilted ridges and planes beneath his shirt where it was drawn taut across the curve of his back by his bent position in the chair. He rose with an explosive motion, pacing to the window.

"Cheer me up, Alan, boy. Tell me a joke, give me a laugh. I'm in the deepest, blackest bog you ever pulled a dogie out of."

The husky vibrations of his voice tugged at small wild things in Craig. He stared up at the tight, pinched furrows forming deeply on either side of Bowie's mouth, as if from some unrelenting compression of the lips.

"You know I never did collect jokes, Bowie," he said. "I'll examine you, if you want."

Bowie's steady, bitter glare out through the window gave a sense of irrelevancy to his words. "You a good doctor, Alan?"

"I try to be, Bowie."

"There isn't anything wrong with me," said Bowie in a sudden, passionate burst. He slapped a hand disgustedly across the tight, California foxed pants he wore, stuffed into the sloppy old boots from Justin's bench. "I never had a sick day in my life, and you know it."

"Nothing wrong physically, you mean."

"That's what I mean."

Craig looked idly around the room, the faded green-gold of the old Navajo blanket thrown across the cot at one side, the worn, scarred cartridge belt and holster lying atop this, containing the Paterson conversion Craig remembered so well, its ivory butt yellow and polished with age and use.

"I was sort of surprised at the Coronet," he said. "For such a big man, you don't run much to display, do you, Bowie?"

"I guess I've been working so hard to get things organized, I haven't had much time for the house. Man makes his barns weatherproof before his home in this country, Alan. You know that."

"And when he's got the barns all finished, what does he do?" This caused Bowie to turn about, those hazelnut lights kindling in his eyes in some transitory speculation. "You used to be happy with just one horse, Bowie. You got so many now I'll bet you couldn't count them. Does it worry you a lot, trying to decide which one to step up on?"

Bowie stared at him a moment longer, anger struggling with something else in his face. Then he turned away, his words thin with cynicism. "Doctor Craig, the armchair philosopher."

"Sorry. I'm not doing much to cheer you up, am I? How about the time we switched the colt Grady's mare had just dropped for a suckling calf, and Grady thought it had really

71

come out of his horse?"

Bowie stood staring out the window so long without reaction that Craig thought it had not registered. Then he saw the little ripple across the man's back beneath his dirty denim vest, and the lifting of the shoulders. Finally Bowie's head was thrown back in that laugh Craig could never forget, as rarely as it had come, wild and pealing as the howl of a coyote, rolling up out of the droll, hidden depths of the man to tickle the air for an instant.

"You're the only one that could do it, Alan!" shouted Bowie, still shaking with the laugh. "Nobody here goes back that far, not even Evan Fox. Tell me another one, Alan."

"How about the night we thought the polecat was an Indian?"

Bowie wheeled about violently, his facile lips stretched back flat against strong teeth, and for a moment Craig thought he would laugh again. Then it left him, swept away by that savage, bitter expression that came back into his face like the turbid wash of flood tide.

"Hell," he said, in a vicious, guttural voice, and turned back to stare out the window.

Craig watched the stiff, unrelenting line of his back, trying to find what had happened to this man he had thought he knew so well. Finally he broke the silence. "How long have you been in the dumps?"

Bowie did not answer for a space. "Couple of days," he said at last. "Feel so snaky I can't even eat."

"Happened before?"

"Yeah. All the time. Like the ague, comes around every year."

"More often than that."

"Okay. More often."

"Whenever you're crossed?"

"Sometimes. Sometimes not."

"Who crossed you this time?"

"Alan Craig."

After that, the silence settled between them again, filled with tension that had been so foreign to their friendship before. Finally Bowie's great, lanky frame lifted with an indrawn breath, and he turned slowly, leaning back against the window sill to place both hands upon it, palms down.

"Why did you do it, Alan? Why did you go up to Jada MacQueen's?"

"His boy would have died, Bowie," Craig told him quietly.

"Good riddance."

"You don't mean that."

Bowie walked across the room in that restless, vicious stride, wheeling at the desk, bringing his hand across its top as he did, to sweep papers and inkwell off onto the floor in a savage, heedless anger.

"You saw what he's doing to the country," he snarled, facing directly toward Craig and fixing him with his eyes. "You passed the old Scissors. Nothing left. Silt five feet deep over the whole thing. All that wild hay on the lower pastures covered. A dozen spreads along the upper Fisher have had to close their books because of MacQueen. Every drop of water polluted with his tailings and muck. I've had cows die on the water that comes down the Fisher now, Alan."

"I heard you tried to talk it over."

"Sure we did. Some plan about channeling all his tailings into one watercourse and letting that carry it out the valley. But he wanted the Fisher. Can you imagine that? What would it leave us?"

"Bull River?"

"Oh." Bowie waved his hand in a hard, bitter "what the hell?"

"And when it finally came down to terms, what did you offer him?"

"You're riding me again, Craig."

"Shall we go back to the jokes?"

"I offered him Meadow Creek."

It came from Bowie in a biting, offhand way. Craig stared at him without answering, unable to keep the faint, twisting smile off his lips. Bowie turned to him, brows pulling together over his eyes as he saw it.

"Well?" he demanded.

"You know as well as I do, Meadow Creek is ten miles off any of his workings," said Craig. "He'd have to flume every bit of his débris over two ridges. I don't wonder he didn't come to terms."

"No matter." That sense of heedless irrelevance entered Bowie again as he said it, all the anger seeming to be gone from him. He turned away, pacing toward the window. "We've got him now, Alan. I'm sorry about Evan and Ingo the other day. I told them to bring you here, that's all. I didn't mean a fight. You'll forgive me?"

"I told Evan I couldn't believe it was your idea."

"Good boy, good boy." Bowie struck the sill with his open palm. "And now, when that kid starts bellyaching again, watch Jada come to us on his knees. He'd change the map of the world for his boy."

"What do you mean, when he starts bellyaching?"

"When they need you again," said Bowie, whirling toward him, a strange, savage eagerness in the brilliant little lights flashing through his eyes. "You're the only doctor in a hundred miles, Alan. We've got that stove-up 'Forty-Niner just where it hurts. So you operated on the kid. I'll never forget that. Maybe it's better you kept him alive. He's the best lever in the world. He'll need a lot of attention after an operation, won't he, Alan, attention only you can give? When it comes to Jada moving down off the mountain or his kid dying, you know which he'll choose. I've been waiting for something like this for a long time, Alan."

Craig stared at him, struggling to take the words at their face value, unable to grasp completely what he was seeing. He shook his head from side to side, still gazing at Bowie. "You really must have been king around here a long while."

"What's that?"

"You take it so much for granted that I've come here to do your bidding, Bowie."

The man stared at him, with the understanding filling his eyes in a slow, turgid wave. Craig expected that violent anger again. Instead, Bowie put his hands on the sill once more, settling his weight down against them.

"And you haven't come to do my bidding?" said Bowie.

"Didn't Evan Fox tell you what I said?"

"Word for word."

"That's where I stand, then, Bowie. I came back to doctor anybody who needs me. You, Jada MacQueen, anybody."

"Why are you here, then?" asked Bowie slowly.

"Don't you know?"

"I'd like it in your words."

"Take the pressure off Donovan and the council. The need for a hospital is obvious enough. They'd do what's necessary if you told them it was all right."

"It would take a long time, even if they were in favor of it," said Bowie. His voice held a strange, philosophic calm, reminiscent of what Craig had known in him before. "You know how these things. . . ."

"It could be hurried along," said Craig.

"It could be hurried along even faster if I built it for you, Alan."

Craig raised his eyes in surprise. Then he made a small, disgusted sound. "I don't need to ask your price."

"Not a price, Alan. A favor. I'll build your hospital if you quit going up to MacQueen's."

"It's not *my* hospital!" said Craig in a passionate voice, rising sharply. "It's for Coffin Gap, the people in it, the people in this whole basin, Bowie. Can't you understand that?"

Bowie did not seem to be listening. "It's funny," he said, looking at Craig, yet not exactly looking at him, something to do with the direction of his eyes, or lack of direction. "It's funny, Alan. I thought the ropes had got twisted somewhere along the line. I thought if you and I could sit down like the old friends we were, and talk it out, we'd be eating our beans off the same plate again."

"I thought the same thing, Bowie."

They stared at each other for a long space of time. At least Craig stared at Bowie. The other man still had that blankness to his eyes, as if looking at something far away. Then he turned, in a quick, vicious motion, to look out the window.

"Get out!" he said in a voice guttural with all the animal capacities in him.

Craig rose slowly. "You're not giving it much chance, Bowie."

"Alan," said Bowie, "I'm asking you . . . I don't want to do anything now. For God's sake, get out!"

The living room was empty when Alan entered it from Bowie's den. He moved across the filthy bear rug, the splintered puncheon flooring beyond, toward the front door, filled with a vague, uncertain sense of some deep hurt at what he had seen in Bowie. This must have shown in his face as he stepped out the door onto the porch, for Nola was sitting there, to one side, and her chin lifted in understanding.

"Has he changed that much?" she asked.

76

He stared at her dimly. "You should know." He found her gaze but could not read it.

"I don't know." She turned partly away from him. "How can one know? He's been this way so long, it seems like it's been always. I wasn't seeing so much of him when you were here, Alan, if you'll remember."

"I remember, Nola," he said quietly.

"Alan," she said, "you do need that hospital, don't you? Donovan was out here the morning you brought Missus Gardener into town. They figured your next move would be a hospital, and Bowie told Donovan to block it. Donovan himself was for it until Bowie turned thumbs down. I've got a little money. Dad had an insurance policy. If it would help . . . ?"

"And when Bowie found that out, what would happen?"

The pupils of her eyes distended, like a cat's just coming into light, and for a moment she was staring beyond Craig. "He wouldn't have to find out," she said then.

"I wouldn't want to put you in that position."

One of her beautiful, dark brows raised with faint inquisition. "Are you sure it's only my position you're worrying about?"

"You're being obscure," he said.

She raised her eyes to his. "Am I, Alan?"

Before he could speak, there was a stirring from within the house. Nola seemed to withdraw, a strange, luminous flash coming to her eyes. She would not meet his gaze as she spoke.

"You'd better go, Alan. There's no point in antagonizing him again."

The ride back to Coffin Gap was full of doubts for Craig. Doubts, and a dull bitterness, and memories. Memories of Bowie in which he sought an answer to what he had seen of the man today.

Bowie's origins had been smoky when he came to work with

77

Craig's father on the Scissors. There was talk of trouble on his back trail, but half the men in the Territory had that following them. A man with his reputation would naturally find trouble wherever he went. That reputation had preceded him to Montana, and it was one of the reasons Bob Craig sought his association.

There had been a lot of trouble getting the Scissors started, what with the sheep war in the Cabinet Basin at that time, and the swarm of rustlers and high-liners who inevitably attended a wide-open range in its beginnings. Much of that trouble stopped when Bowie French became Bob Craig's partner.

Looking back, Craig saw that the hero worship was logical. *He had never tried to deny the attraction such a colorful, reckless figure held for him. But he felt, somehow, that it had never reached him so deeply, so obviously as it had the other boys his age. Even then, if more dimly than now, his eyes had been turned toward another star. He wondered if that was one of the reasons Bowie had accepted him on a more equal plane, though there was ten years' difference in their ages.*

And then there was the gun. It had started more as something to occupy time that winter he and Bowie spent out in the lonely line cabin in the Cabinets. When his father found out, he had urged the boy on. And Bowie had been more than willing to share his skills.

What happened after that was almost inevitable. A man named Christians came down out of the Swans with a mean reputation. He had blotted the Scissors brand on some cattle up in the Cabinets and then drove them into the stockyards at Coffin Gap to sell them under his own brand. Alan had trailed him down and stopped him with the cattle at the head of Cutbank Street. There was one brand Christians hadn't done a very good job on, and the Scissors was still identifiable. Alan wanted to go for the marshal, but Christians didn't give him time.

When it was all over, nobody would come very near Alan Craig.

They gathered around Christians, where he had fallen. He had been the first of the two to reach for his gun, and it wasn't even out of its holster as he lay there, sprawled on his back. So they gathered around him, staring in a strange, furtive awe at the boy who stood a few feet off with the smoking gun yet in his hand, not going very near him. For weeks afterward Craig could not come to town without noticing the groups that broke up along the sidewalk at his approach, and the men who gave him plenty of room when he passed them on the sidewalk.

That brought it down, somehow, to the last day, when Craig had buried his father and sold the Scissors, and it was just the two of them, Bowie and Alan, standing in the dusty, mote-filled shafts of sunlight that slanted through the front room of the ranch house. Bowie was holding out Craig's holstered gun wrapped in its heavy cartridge belt.

"I don't think so, Bowie," Craig had told him. "What place would it have in a doctor's life?"

"A man doesn't drop a thing so easily that he's taken so long to acquire, Alan," Bowie had said. "You'll learn that. If you mean to come back west after you're through medical school, you'd better keep the gun. It's become a greater part of your life than you realize, Alan. They still remember Christians in Coffin Gap. He had a big reputation. They still remember what you did to him. It's spread beyond town. I've heard more than one high-liner talk about it. They won't forget, Alan. It's something you'll have to find out for yourself. . . ."

And Craig had looked at Bowie with a new understanding, remembering how Bowie's name had preceded him into the basin, how it had been there long before the man himself came. It had filled Craig with a trapped, suffocated feeling for a moment. He wondered if a cow felt the same way when it was branded. Then that had passed, and, in a quiet acceptance of the category his own skill had placed him in, he reached out for the gun.

79

The weight of it seemed emphasized against his leg now, as the buckboard thumped down off the Coronet cutoff into Territory Road. And he was thinking that three days ago he had met Evan Fox and Ingo Hubbard on this very road. Evan Fox hadn't forgotten. *Watch his gun, Ingo, watch his gun.* More than nine years, and Evan hadn't forgotten. And Garnet hadn't. Probably none of them had.

Craig had meant to go on up to MacQueen's from the turnoff at Territory Road, but it started to rain, and he headed the mile back to town, meaning to get a full meal under his belt and have his slicker if he meant to go up on the mountain in a storm. He pulled into the livery stable, seeing Harry Fields turn from the rear and come running up the row of softly snorting, stamping animals.

"If you'll give Pepper and Salt something to eat, Harry, I'll be back in an hour."

"Doc, Doc, you got to git out of town quick," broke in Fields.

Craig had stood on the footboards to climb down off the buckboard, but he checked himself there, something chilling the very pit of him. "Why, Harry?"

"Jada MacQueen's boy has died, and Jada is down off the mountain, hunting for you."

Chapter Six

That was a hectic evening for Craig. His first impulse was to go up on the mountain, wanting to know how the boy had died, wanting to know why. But the rainstorm had become too bad for travel; freight wagons were bogged down all along Cutbank, and more than one straggler was coming in on a bareback wagon horse, leaving his rig stranded somewhere out on Territory Road or among the benches westward of town. Gabriel Irish had reached Craig by then and convinced him how fruitless a trip up the mountain would be, if the boy was already dead, and MacQueen was down here anyway.

But that driven desire to find the cause of the boy's death, to hear it first hand, still clawed at Craig. He spent the bulk of the evening ducking in and out of doorways along the rain-drenched sidewalk of the main street, hunting the man who had seen MacQueen. Fields had said it was Campbell, a farmer with a place out beyond Brockhalter's store. Craig finally found him in the harness shop. The man said he had seen MacQueen at Brockhalter's. The miner had come there, gripped with such a terrible rage he could hardly make himself understood. There were others who thought they had seen MacQueen down by the Cutbank Bridge across the Kootenai, but none knew where he was now.

Irish tried to get Craig to leave town, but the doctor would not go. Sooner or later he would have to meet MacQueen. There was no point in running from it. Irish finally persuaded Craig to come to the saloon and try to get some sleep. Craig had been sharing Irish's upstairs room behind the main part of the saloon since Mrs. Gardener had been occupying the room at the Blackhorn. The doctor could not get to sleep, however.

He did not know how long he had tossed, tortured by the thought of Duncan's death, trying fruitlessly to find the answer for it.

Finally he threw off the covers, unable to bear the grinding vortex of his thoughts. He swung his legs to the floor and sought the bedside chair with groping fingers, wondering how long he had been here. He could hear no sounds from the saloon. It must be late. He found his coat hung on the back of the chair and hunted in this for one of the cheroots he had acquired a taste for in college. It was then that the board creaked in the hall outside.

There was something furtive about the sound that brought an impulsive reaction. He was inclined forward, with his hand on the butt of his gun where it lay in its holster on the chair, when the door swung open to cast its streak of illumination across him. The silhouette was Gabriel Irish.

"Jumpy?" asked the man.

Though Craig could not actually see his eyes, he knew they were on that hand, and drew it almost guiltily off the gun.

"Guess so," he said. "What time is it?"

"Three in the morning." Irish sat on the bed beside him. "You'd better let me send one of my gentlemen with you, Alan."

"Where?"

"You've got a call. Some kid came in from the MacBell House. His mother is sick. Sounds like typhoid."

Craig took one look at him, then rose and started to dress. Everywhere he turned, he could not help but look at the strange, exotic objects filling the room — the small Buddha contemplating its jade naval atop an ebony table exquisitely inlaid with ivory, the vicious-looking club of some native design suspended on the wall, the countless arrays of cups and bottles and pottery filling the shelves of the room, inscribed upon in a dozen languages.

82

"Like my little retreat?" asked Irish jauntily.

"Some day you'll have to tell me the story of all those things," said Craig. He nodded at the gaudy plumage on the wall. "Even to the peacock feather."

Irish laughed throatily. "Not the one Sufeja used, Craig. Thought I was kidding, didn't you? It wouldn't work anyway. I tickled hell out of myself and still got drunk."

"How about that knobbed club?"

"A guayacon. I got it off a Chicarato down in Mexico. He tried to kill me with it when I claimed the peyote they drink was hogwash. He gave it to me after I mixed him a real drink."

Craig was almost finished dressing now, and he found his eyes on the long-necked bottle covered with quilted straw that stood alone on one shelf. "That seems to have a place of honor."

"It's a *caraba*, Alan," said Irish. "A Persian wine bottle. I got it at Naishapur when I visited the tomb of Omar Khayyam. I stayed with an old innkeeper there. He was quite a philosopher. He said man was a lonely wanderer, coming into contact with thousands of people during his life . . . like the wind lifts the dust only to drop it again . . . yet knowing a true affinity, a feeling of real kinship with only one or two of those people in all that time."

"There's truth in that," Craig murmured.

"You feel it, too?" Irish seemed mildly surprised. Then he smiled in a sad, pleased way. "The innkeeper gave me the wine bottle. He told me that whenever I crossed the trail of someone with whom I found this affinity, I should drink with him from the *caraba*."

"How long ago was that?" said Craig.

"Years ago."

"It looks like it's still full."

"It is, Alan."

Craig turned sharply to the man, touched by something

indescribably lonely. The ruddy, cheerful urbanity had slipped off Irish's face. His eyes seemed focused on something beyond the confines of the room. It gave Craig the sense of a new insight into the man. Before the feeling could develop, Irish became aware of Craig's attention on him and raised his head with a small start. A flutter of embarrassment slipped through his eyes. That faded when the return of the suave, affable geniality to which Craig was so accustomed dropped like a veil over this brief glimpse into the lost part of the man. Irish waved his hand at the room.

"There you have the man," he said in jaunty cynicism, calculated to break the mood. "The soul of a prince in the body of a peasant. A tragic story, really. I often cry in my beer when I'm alone."

Craig felt a stab of embarrassment, the discomfort men feel when they get too close to sentiment. He turned away to finish his dressing, bothered by what he had seen, wishing that he had time right now to follow it up. He got his coat, and they went downstairs in that uncomfortable silence. The boy was in the main part of the saloon, a shivering urchin in tattered clothes, face obscured by the sodden wrapper thrown over his head. Irish roused Gentleman George from the sleeping quarters behind the bar.

He actually had about as much claim to the title of "gentleman" as a gorilla. He was a prodigious, shuffling beast of a man, shrugging uncomfortably in a castoff Army greatcoat. One of his ears had been sliced off in some former fight, and the flesh across his heavy, prominent cheekbones was darkened by bruises that would never heal.

The three of them ducked down the street, under overhangs and into doorways, to the livery stable. Harry Fields had given Craig a key to his side door for emergencies, and the doctor let himself in to harness up Salt and Pepper with the help of the boy and Gentleman George.

The spiderwebbed ruts filling the street outside were brimming with tarnished water, mottled by the minute, quicksilver whirlpools brought to life by the incessant beat of rain. There was something sinister about the viscid, sucking sound made by the passage of wheels through the mud. By the time they reached the turnoff at Territory Road, Craig became aware of George's head turning slowly from side to side. The muffled rattle of rain on the man's hatbrim ceased as he turned his face upward.

"What is it?" Craig asked him.

"You hear something, Doc?"

Craig felt his legs press into the seat with a stiffening tension. His own head turned from side to side, staring into the desolate shadows pocketing the sidewalks under the wooden overhangs and in between the buildings. He listened intently but could hear nothing over the unending tattoo of rain. He turned again to George, who was still staring about him. Craig realized the man was not looking at anything in particular. His gaze was directed upward in a vague, awed way.

"What does it sound like?" asked Craig.

"Like buzzin'," answered the man. His jaw dropped bucolically. "Like a little somethin' buzzin'."

Craig took up the slack in the reins, urging his horses ahead, studying the man closely. "You been in a lot of fights, George?"

"Yeah," the man grinned, turning to him. "You should 'a' seen me when I was in Butte. They had a driller there called The Duke. They said he. . . ."

"Take a lot of punches, George?" asked Craig.

"Give a lot, too," grinned the man. "You'll be all right with me tonight, Doc. Irish wanted to send Gentleman Jack, but he ain't no good. All he can do is swing a pool cue. . . ." He broke off again to stare around.

Craig saw the boy, on the other side of the seat, looking up at George with wondering eyes. They were well down Territory Road now, with the MacBell House appearing through the smoky fog of rain ahead, a brooding, somber structure, its tin gutters rattling in raucous protest at the downpour.

The boy jumped from the buckboard before Craig had halted it, ducking for the stairway. Craig got off and hitched his team to the rusty tie ring in the old iron post, then he got his bag.

Gentleman George trailed him by a few feet, with the boy already out of sight in the stairway. It gave Craig the feel of approaching the place alone, bringing the past up suddenly, with the faces, a bobbing, burgeoning circle of them, surrounding him and that hand clutching his bag. Something welled up in him approaching fear, and he almost stopped. Then the steady, plodding, sucking sound of Gentleman George just behind brought him out of it, and he shrugged his shoulders irritably in the slicker.

At the mouth of the stairway something else entered his mind, more of the present, and he did halt this time, staring up into the pitch blackness. He could hear the boy's footsteps, receding up the creaking old boards. Without thinking, he found his hand beneath the slicker, hitching his gun a little farther around.

"Something wrong?" George wanted to know.

"Nothing," said Craig. "Let's go."

His own weight added to that haunted creaking brought from the stairs by the boy above. He put his hand against the wall to guide himself. Then his was the only sound, and he realized the boy must have reached the landing. An instant later the boy's cry came.

"Doctor!"

It was shrill and frightened, causing Craig's head to lift sharply to the sound. Then Gentleman George grunted heavily from behind, and Craig could not help turning toward the man. The faint backlight from outside was blocked off by the struggling surge of figures down there. At the same time the stairs shuddered with the hurtling racket of someone coming down from above. The doctor was only whirled part way back when the weight struck him, an immense weight, prodigious with bone and beef. Carrying him back against the wall in stunning impact. Knocking his head against the boards in a glancing blow.

His bag out of his hands, he sought desperately to keep his balance. To get his gun free. His fighting, struggling feet stumbled backward down the stairs. Then that body struck him again from above, coming on after him.

This time it knocked him off his feet. He doubled over sideways to hit the opposite wall with his shoulder. He caromed off that to strike the steps on the flat of his back. His heels came over his head in a flopping motion over which he had no control. Then he came over onto his belly, head twisted grotesquely beneath him. A vicious kick caught Craig under the shoulder, sending him on down the remaining steps to heap up on the landing, brought to a stop by a body. He made a violent effort to squirm into a position where he could get his feet under him. This brought Gentleman George's bloody, unconscious face up against his, there on the dank, sodden floor of the entrance way. As he started to rise, the man from above was on him again, kicking.

Craig's whole body jerked. He heard the sound of it, as if outside himself. The heavy, sickening impact of boot into flesh and bone. It brought a gasping shout of pain from him. He was carried backward off Gentleman George's huddled body in a flopping, writhing way to tumble out of the entrance into the mud outside.

Dazed, nauseated with the pain, he still had enough presence of mind to come to a stop in such a position that he could get his feet beneath him. He caught the side of the house with his left hand, pushing himself onto one knee and fumbling under his slicker for the gun. He could see that it was Jada MacQueen now, like the warped, exaggerated vision of some nightmare, burgeoning out of the doorway from the stairs and shouting: "Get that gun, Jack, and get it good."

With his hand still under the coat Craig's elbow was caught from behind, his whole arm pulled around in a hammerlock that bent him forward on his knee. He felt his slicker torn up, a sharp, brutal tug at his waist as the gun was yanked free of the holster. Bent forward that way, he could not see Jada. But he knew there was another kick coming. And he knew, just as certainly, that he was not meant to get out of this alive. In a spasm of utter desperation, knowing it would break his arm but, knowing also, that it was the only way he could avoid MacQueen's kick, he lunged forward against that hammerlock, doubling over.

He felt the terrible, sucking pull of the arm as it jerked from the shoulder socket. Then the crack of bone. His own scream blotted that out. But with some other dim, distant consciousness beyond the pain he felt Cousin Jack pulled over his shoulder by that lunge, and knew MacQueen's kick had missed him. He caught Cousin Jack with his free arm and yanked him on over into the mud. With a vague sense of where the man's head was, he threw the weight of his body forward, seeking it with his knee.

He felt the writhe of muscle against his shin bone as he bore down on the man's chest. He moved the leg up in a vicious, jerking motion, bringing the knee down fully into Jack's face. He heard the gurgling sound Jack made, felt the slippery roll of cheek and brow beneath his knee, as the man tried to get his head out from beneath it.

Right arm dangling uselessly at his side, he caught the man's muddy hair with his free hand, jerking the face back under him, and coming down into it with his knee once more. At the same time Jada was on Craig again. Craig had no coherent sense of the man in those final moments. His consciousness was of fists and boots and the vagrant, nauseating reek of whiskey and tobacco and heated sweat. His head was jerked from one side to the other, his body torn back off Cousin Jack by a kick. He sprawled back into the mud with Jada following him.

He rolled over and came to his knees to meet the man. Jada's boot caught him in the ribs. He grunted with all the deep, blinding pain of it, yet still managed to hook the ankle in his elbow before it knocked him back. Before Jada could pull free, he was up against the man, still on his knees, with his face against MacQueen's stinking belly. He let go the man's legs to strike for the groin, deliberately, viciously.

Jada made a sick, gasping sound, and doubled over, pawing at him. This pinned Craig's free arm between them. He tried to twist out, but MacQueen's whole body bore him backwards. Then he heard some small, shuffling sound behind him and realized it was Cousin Jack. The man had not been able to gain his feet. He was coming toward Craig from behind on his hands and knees, face dripping blood and muck and rain water. The utter wordlessness of the whole struggle was the most terrible part. Like some prehistoric animal, groveling around in the pristine slime of a nascent world, blinking those great, sloth-like eyes, making small, guttural sounds of effort, Cousin Jack reached Craig, raising up off his hands to free his weight from them, and striking.

The blow caught Craig on the side of the head, knocking him back into MacQueen. At the same moment MacQueen brought his knee up into the doctor's face. There was no more sight left to Craig after that. With his face buried against Mac-

Queen, he heard their forced, bestial sounds, their grunts, the sucking, sloppy shift of their bodies in the mud, the sodden sound of their blows. Then there was no more sound left to him. Only the last, inchoate vestiges of some sense he could not identify. And then, no sense at all, but thought, the last knowledge of any kind he would have on earth. *So this is the way it feels to die.*

Chapter Seven

First, there was only blackness. Like cotton. All around him, like black, lightless cotton, suffocating, pillowing, lacking all substance as he had known it, yet pressing in on him with a weight he could not bear. Then pinpoints of light began to appear in the night. Small and winking. Bright and small and winking. And sounds. Faint, maddening susurrations that rose and fell like a restless tide. Finally contact. Something seemed to be crawling all over him. It made him squirm and open his eyes. He was under water. There were pallid, formless shapes floating around him. One began to take shape. Huge eyes. Huge blinking eyes. A gaping red mouth. White teeth in a gaping red mouth. Gabriel Irish.

"Coming around, Alan? It's about time."

Craig was out of the water now. He had heard a patient describe the same symptoms upon recovering from ether. But he had not been under an anesthetic. He moved his head, and that sent pain shooting up his neck.

"I'm in your room?" His voice seemed to float above him.

"You sure are."

"Will you put a shade over the light or something?"

"That's the sun."

"You mean it's tomorrow?"

"That's right. About three o'clock in the afternoon . . . tomorrow."

Craig sighed heavily with the full return of consciousness. "How did I get here, Irish? They were set to kill me."

"Missus Mullin's kid saved your life. He ran all the way back here. My gentlemen and I arrived on the scene as Jada Mac-Queen was getting set to stamp your head in. We managed to prevent that, but we couldn't hold them. I never saw a man like that MacQueen. How did you ever last as long as you did?"

"I'll never know," groaned Craig. He started moving experimentally. He ached all over. The shooting pains started when he put any weight on his right side, and he guessed that meant broken ribs. Then his left. This brought more pain, so violent he could not help gasping.

"Watch that arm," said Irish. "I think it's broken."

"I imagine. Anybody set it?"

"You're the only doctor around here, Alan."

"Help me sit up, then, will you? I'd like to look over the damage."

He had been lying with his head thrown back, eyes closed, after that first look at Irish. But now, as Irish bent to lift him, he felt another hand slip under his other arm. He opened his eyes once more. It was Nola. She was in black taffeta that seemed to echo the slightest movement of her body with a muted sibilance. The lace scarf thrown over her head gave her face a haunted, Oriental cast.

"Bowie know you're here?" he asked.

"No," she told him.

"Aren't you sort of taking a chance?"

She did not actually look away, but some blankness entered her eyes, hiding whatever lay behind, almost as if she had turned aside to do so. Then this faded, and she put a hand softly on his wrist.

"I had to come. Dunnymead was in town today. He brought the news back. I had to see that you're all right."

"Thanks, Nola," he said. He gazed at her a moment longer, then turned to unwrap the awkward sling and bandages they had put on his arm. It was swollen and discolored, tender to the touch.

"Pott's fracture," he murmured.

Irish frowned. "What?"

"The fibula," answered Craig absently, studying his arm. "Named after the way Percival Pott broke it when his horse threw him. English physician."

"My God," said Irish. "They even name something like that after a man?"

"Why not?" shrugged Craig. "What about Tom Collins?"

"All right, all right," chuckled Irish. Then he sobered again. "What has to be done, Alan?"

"I'll have to set it myself." Craig moved his shoulder experimentally, wincing at the pain it brought to his lower arm. "Thought I'd have to reduce a dislocation, too. When I pulled Jack off me, it felt like my shoulder went, but apparently it didn't come clear out. If you'll get a couple of your gentlemen to hold me, we can start. I guess you'd better go outside, Nola."

"I want to help, Alan."

"I think you'd better go. It's going to be messy."

"My uncle was gored by a bull when I was thirteen. I helped him hold his intestines in for three hours while somebody went for a doctor."

Craig could not hide his surprise as he stared at her. It had held all the sober naïveté of a child's recital. There was little expression in her face now, as she gazed at him, wide-eyed and waiting. Irish chuckled again in that wry, raffish way.

"I think she'd probably be better than any of my gentlemen, Alan."

"All right, Nola," Craig told her. "Clear that side table and bring it over here. I'm going to lay my arm across it. You hold the table steady. Irish, you take me by the elbow in one hand, and by the upper arm with the other. No matter how I jerk, keep my forearm flat on the table."

There was something strained about their subdued movements. Then he seemed to become more conscious of their breathing. It brought memory of that operation at MacQueen's. *Why is it always this way in a moment like this?* His own breathing had a husky, repressed tone. Irish was almost wheezing. Only Nola's was natural, almost soothing in its steady susurration.

Calmly she cleared the table off, bringing it over to the bed. Then she helped him lay his forearm flat across its surface.

"Keep your weight centered against me," Craig told Irish. He was sweating now. "Don't let go under any circumstances." He felt sick at his stomach. "Are you ready?"

It took him three attempts to get it set. He could not help jerking with the pain the first time, and Irish grunted with his effort of maintaining the grip. He passed out the second time and came to with the fiery, choking burn of whiskey in his mouth. After it was over, he lay back, trembling and weak. Nola began to wash his face with a cloth from the wash bowl that had stood on the table. When he was able, he directed them in making a splint for the arm, and in tending to his other wounds and bruises, and binding up his broken ribs. He was surprised at Nola's efficiency, at how quickly she acquired the skill in dressing and bandaging. When it was finished, Irish told them he would go downstairs to get a meal for Craig. Nola seated herself on a chair beside the bed, and remained there silently. He turned his head toward her, speaking weakly.

"My gratitude, Nola."

"I don't want that."

"What do you want?"

"Only to help you, Alan. You're so alone in this town."

He studied her dark, shadowed face, asking quietly, "Did you come in the front way, Nola?"

She met his eyes squarely, answering without hesitation. "No, Alan. The back way."

"Nola" — he rolled over slightly in order to look at her more

94

squarely — "do you think that will be any good for either of us, in the end?"

"It's not a matter of bad or good, Alan. When I heard you were hurt, I didn't think about that at all. I just knew I had to come and see you. And they did beat you so terribly, Alan."

He seemed to catch a faint tremor in her voice on the last words. He stared up at her face, waiting for the emotion to fulfill itself. But it seemed checked by something, to hover just behind the stirred darkness of her eyes, waiting for something. He knew what it was now. She wanted some sign from him, some recognition. He turned his face restlessly away, reluctant to meet that expression in her eyes, unwilling to give any sign. She was another man's wife. Yet, somehow, it went deeper than that. It went down to his own feelings that he could not yet define. He stirred, oddly irritated.

"You and Bowie mustn't have much left," he murmured, still turned away from her.

"You mean to come to you, like this?"

"A woman doesn't love one man and go to another, Nola."

He heard the rustle of her dress as she rose. It whispered across the room and stopped, and he knew she must be standing by the shelves, looking at those myriad, strange bottles and jugs Irish had collected, without actually seeing them.

"I'll admit it then, Alan," she said in a deep, resigned way. "Bowie and I don't have much left."

"When did his moods start?"

"Always the doctor, aren't you?"

"It goes beyond that."

"I'm sorry," she said. "I didn't notice the moods at first. I guess he was keeping them from me. He used to disappear three or four days at a time. I thought he was just out with the cattle. Then he didn't bother disappearing, or trying to hide the moods from me. He locked himself in his room. I can't understand it, Alan. He seems like a crazy person when he goes into one of those rages."

"I've been trying to figure it out since I saw him. Did he ever tell you much of his past, Nola?"

"Very little."

"He never told me, either. As much time as we spent with each other, I had to piece it together from what he dropped, and what I heard about him. He must have been very poor when he was a kid. I know his mother died when they were kicked out in a Texas norther because they couldn't pay their rent. I got the idea his father committed suicide later because he was unable to support the kids. Bowie was about ten at the time. It would have been hard enough for a man, grubbing through those years after the war. Think what it could mean to a kid of ten, without any people? It must have left a pretty bitter mark."

"It's funny," she said. "I never got any of that. His own wife . . . and I never got any of it. I guess you were closer to him than any of us, Alan."

It filled Craig with a vague sadness. "Bowie and I used to sit up on top of the Cabinets and look at this basin. I can remember the hungry look he got in his face. Like a starving man watching food that wasn't his. I didn't realize what that meant at the time. Or understand why he'd take the butt of his cigarette, instead of throwing it away, and unroll the paper and pour the tobacco in his pouch." Craig turned his head to look at her. "Does he still save buttons?"

"He's got a drawer full," she said.

"That's what I mean," Craig told her. "Those things never fitted into the reckless, devil-may-care picture Bowie made for most people. I thought they were just quirks at the time. They were, all right. Quirks of a man who's had a fear of poverty instilled in him so deeply he can never forget it. I was surprised at the state he'd let your home ranch degenerate into. I guess he's been clawing so hard for more, he hasn't had time for repairs."

"I think it's more than that. I think he's just too tight-fisted to spend the money. There's something miserly about it."

"Did it ever strike you that those rages don't come every time Bowie is crossed?" asked Craig. "I've seen a man hit Bowie and leave him cold as ice. Could it be that only something bearing on that fear of poverty brings on the temper? It came when I went up to MacQueen's against Bowie's wishes. The silt from this hydraulicking threatens Coronet. Coronet is the bulwark Bowie's sweated and slaved and fought to build between himself and that poverty. He thought he could use me as a lever to stop MacQueen's hydraulicking, and I crossed him up. And he threw a rage."

"Perhaps you're right. It does follow sort of a pattern. Bowie's had lots of fights with the crew. That never left him in one of those moods."

"I noticed some vented Cocked Hat brands on a cut of cattle the day I went out there. They'd been changed to Coronet."

"We did that to all Dad's cattle after I married Bowie. We thought it would save a lot of work for the crews. If we'd left it Cocked Hat, they would have had to put a Coronet road brand on everything we drove to market anyway, and you know what a job that would be with the number of cattle Bowie's running now."

"Yes, I imagine."

The tone of his voice brought her eyes sharply to his face. "What are you thinking, Alan?"

He was staring thoughtfully at the ceiling. "Were you completely in accord with his plan for changing the brands at first?"

"We discussed it thoroughly."

"You mean he kept prodding you till you agreed?"

"All right." Her shrug was almost sullen. "You will have to admit the reason was valid."

"Maybe he even threw a rage when you wouldn't agree right away."

"No," she said. "He didn't."

"You said he hid the rages from you at first. Maybe until after he had gotten you to agree on the switch of brands."

She came back to the bed, staring down at him. "Alan, what are you thinking?"

He stirred restlessly, avoiding her eyes, unwilling to put it into words yet. "I don't know, Nola. Maybe I've gone too far trying to figure this thing out. It's hit me low. I came back expecting a pretty big welcome from Bowie. Seeing him like this, well. . . ."

"Oh, let's stop this," she told him. "Can't we talk about something cheerful?" She turned from side to side as if seeking some escape, and her eyes settled on a package by the foot of the bed. She bent to pick it up. "This came from the East for you on the morning stage."

Craig stared at it somberly, knowing what it was. Finally he nodded for her to unwrap it. Her fingers held swift, firm deftness, untying the cord, and taking off the heavy paper. She picked the wadding from inside the box to reveal the shining instruments, with their ring handles and ratchet locks.

"Looks like scissors," she murmured, moving one curiously.

"Halsted clamps," he said. The weary, metallic tone of his voice drew her gaze to his face. He was too weak, too tired to try and veil the discouragement there.

"What is it, Alan? What are they for?"

"They're hemostats, Nola, for clamping arteries in an operation."

"Oh." It left her in whispered understanding. Still holding the box, she sat down on the bed, watching him. "And you didn't have them with the MacQueen boy, is that it?"

"I had to use a tenaculum. It's more awkward, leaves a hole in the vessel."

"And you think that caused his death?"

Craig moved from side to side in the beginnings of that torture he had first known upon hearing of Duncan's death. "I don't know. I don't know. If I could only have seen him, Nola, if I could only talk to Jada or Garnet. I can't believe it was my sutures. They were strong enough to hold under ordinary circumstances. I can't even believe it was infection. I was so careful to sterilize it all."

"Alan, Alan" — she was beside his head now, stroking it with her hand — "you've got to stop worrying about it. I know what a terrible thing your first death must be, but you can't be to blame. You tried your best. Please stop worrying."

"I can't. I've got to know. I want you to get some books for me at the office. *Body Temperature and Disease*. Wanderlich is the author. Then there's one by Koch. *Etiology of Wound Infection*."

"I thought you said it couldn't be infection?"

"How can I know for sure, Nola? Maybe it was my carbolic. Mattens said Lister had gotten it down to a five percent solution, but. . . ."

She grasped his good arm as he began tossing again, forcing him back. "I'll get your books. I'll get your books. But can't you wait till tomorrow? You're so weak now. It will only upset you worse. Please, Alan."

There was something about her voice that soothed him. After he quieted, she sat studying him for a long while. He closed his eyes, trying to block it from his mind. But the torment would not go.

"Maybe you'd like to talk," she said at last. "You might as well do that as lie there and think about it." He opened his eyes once more to stare at her, not quite understanding.

She rose in a restlessness of her own, moving to stare out the window at the squalid back alley. Then she said: "I got sick when I went East with Dad and had to spend a couple of months at the University Hospital in Pennsylvania. I saw enough of those internes, Alan. They filled the day with talk. Twenty-four hours isn't enough, is it? I guess there aren't many other professions in which a man can get so wrapped up. It must be stifling to be cut off so abruptly from that world. There isn't a soul out here, is there? You talk all day, but you don't really *talk*. Not the way you'd like to. You even discuss medicine all day. And yet you don't discuss it at all. Telling some old woman how many pink pills to take, and how many blue ones. Trying to beat it through some fool's head that flies get in unless the windows are screened. That isn't really talking at all, is it?"

He found his eyes open once more, staring at her.

She faced about to nod at him. "That's the way it is, isn't it? Till you've got so much bottled up inside you, it's going to explode or something. Who's this Mattens, now?"

"I worked under him at Massachusetts General. He'd spent a couple of years with Lister in the Glasgow Royal Infirmary."

"I thought they weren't taking to Lister much over here?"

"I don't know why," Craig told her. "They've proved the value of his techniques so conclusively in Europe. Nessbaum's hospital in Munich, for instance. Gangrene and erysipelas used to develop in eighty percent of all the wounds. When Nessbaum adopted Lister's techniques in Eighteen Seventy-Five, both gangrene and erysipelas disappeared completely. That's why I can't understand Duncan MacQueen's death. Even under those crude conditions I should have been able to reduce the danger of infection to a very small percent. If I made a mistake somewhere, I want to know. I've got to know. You can understand?"

He was amazed at the grasp she displayed. He could talk

with her on the level he would use with another doctor. He wore himself out talking, not only about the MacQueen operation, but all the things he had come up against since he had arrived here, all the frustrations and defeats and harrying little questions of medicine which he had been forced to keep within himself. Finally, too tired to go on, he sank back into the bed, smiling ruefully at her.

"I didn't mean to talk your arm off, Nola."

Before she could answer, there was a knock at the door, and Irish came in with a tray, chuckling throatily. "*Crêpes au Kirsch*, Alan. *Bouillabaise, oeufs al rancho*. A meal fit for a potentate."

Nola rose, and her eyes were on the man's face in that moment. Irish was turned aside, setting the tray down, but Craig sensed the man's awareness of that glance. His cheeks seemed to flatten slightly with some tension of the muscles along his jaw. Then Nola turned to Craig.

"I'll be going, Alan. I'll bring your books to you the next time I come."

There was nothing but that genial smile on Irish's face as he bowed Nola out. It faded, however, as he stood at the door, watching her descend the stairs.

"I feel a saying coming on," he murmured.

Craig studied his face, disturbed by the expression it conveyed. There was no humor left. The roguish light in Irish's eyes had fled before a strange, contradictory mixture of pity and deviltry.

"Maybe you'd better not quote it, Irish."

There was something sharp, almost startled, in the way Irish turned to look at him. His eyes held Craig's for only a moment. Then, in vague, undefined guilt, they dropped. "I suppose you're right. You're an authority on medicine. I'm an authority on drinking. Nobody's an authority on women."

Chapter Eight

Craig spent a week in bed, recovering from the beating, and then could no longer ignore the demands for him. He was stiff and weak his first day up, with his ribs still bound tightly and his arm in a sling. He returned late in the afternoon, stupefied with exhaustion and pain, and threw himself back into bed. But the heat of coming summer was already filling the land, and the incidence of typhoid was rising. He could not ignore the dozen new cases to be taken care of, and rose the next morning to start the weary rounds again.

Irish cared for him like a mother, undressing him at night when he returned too played out to do it himself, keeping a hot meal waiting for him no matter when he came in. Though Asa Gardener's wife was getting well, she was still in Craig's room at the Blackhorn, and he was staying at the saloon. Nobody else at the Blackhorn had contracted typhoid, and Marcus had made no further move to have her evicted. It was about a week after he got out of bed for good that Craig came back to the Nebuchadnezzar one afternoon to find immense glass bowls set at either end of the long bar, already partly filled with coins. He made his way through the early crowd to the kitchen at the rear. It was not large enough to serve the whole saloon, but the cooking for Irish and the help was done here. It was a humid, poorly ventilated room with a great wood stove at one side and a long plank table at the other. When Irish caught sight of Craig, he went to the stove and began to ladle stew into a soup dish. Craig slipped out of his coat and seated himself wearily on a bench by the table.

"What are the bowls out there for, Irish?"

"Collection for illegitimate bartenders and disabled short-card dealers," grinned Irish, his eyes twinkling. Then he turned with the stew and saw how tired Craig was. "I'm sorry, Alan," he said, coming over to put the bowl down. "A bunch of the townsmen decided we needed a hospital whether Mayor Donovan thought so or not. The saloon keepers have agreed to up the price of their drinks ten percent and put that in the kitty. Those bowls are the collection plate. Anything else my inebriate patrons want to donate is welcome, too."

Craig stared up at him. "But that won't begin to pay. . . ."

"It will *begin* to pay for the hospital," said Irish. "That's just it. We realize there have to be other sources. Have you ever thought of the dirt farmers in Cabinet Basin? This battle between the lowlanders and MacQueen may have allied the cattlemen and the farmers temporarily, but basically they've always been bitterly opposed to each other. In normal times you're either with the farmers or with the beef interests. By now it's pretty obvious you aren't playing along with Bowie. That about makes you a candidate for the farm ticket. This typhoid's touched the outlying districts hard enough to scare them and start them thinking. If there were to be a meeting of farmers, and you were to speak to them, I think you could make them see the necessity for a hospital. A donation from them would mean a lot."

"I suppose the same group of public-spirited citizens who concocted the glass bowl idea would arrange for a meeting with the farmers," said Craig.

"It could be done," nodded Irish.

"Just who are these citizens, Gabriel?"

"Well. . . ." He hesitated, clearing his throat.

"Gabriel Irish, Gabriel Irish, and Gabriel Irish?" asked Craig.

Their eyes met. Irish tried to suppress his sheepish grin. Then they both started chuckling. They were stopped by Gentleman George, coming in from the saloon to tell Craig that he had an urgent call down on Territory Road.

Craig rose tiredly. "Thanks, George. How's the head?"

The man looked surprised. Then he grinned broadly. "Fine, Doc. I'll bet it heals before your arm does. That Cousin Jack, he don't pack much of a wallop. Just let me at him again. Did you ever hear how I handled The Duke up at Butte?" He broke off to lift his head and stare around the room. A frown corrugated his simian brow.

"Yes, George, yes, yes," said Irish indulgently. "Lot of flies in here. We'll have to do something about it." He turned to Craig. "Better take him with you."

Craig shook his head, grinning at Irish. "I can't keep taking your house men on every little call. You're short-handed as it is. MacQueen wouldn't dare come that near town in broad daylight. This is just around the corner now, and I'll be back before dark."

It was a delivery in one of the miners' cabins adjacent to the MacBell House. There was no trouble, and Craig finished while it was still afternoon. He was climbing into his buckboard when the wagon appeared down the road, drawn by a team of heavy, plodding Percherons. Craig could see that the pale, shimmering heap of grain did not even half fill the great, flare-boarded grain tank of the other wagon. The driver pulled his outfit over to Craig, halting it there, a tall, gaunt, bony man with the chronic weariness of ceaseless labor in his stooped shoulders and dull eyes. Wind and weather and a lifetime of grubbing at the soil had turned his flesh the color and texture of the land itself, filling it with the deep gnarled seams of a haphazardly furrowed field.

"You the doc?" he asked.

Craig nodded.

"I was just by Brockhalter's. He told me to look you up if I went to town. His wife's bad off."

"I'll go up there." Craig's eyes were still on the grain, and he inclined his head toward the tank. "Been a dry year?"

"Dry, hell," said the man in a deep, ugly bitterness. "It's been a wet year. And every rain floods them rivers and carries MacQueen's tailings across our land. Another season like this, and I won't have any crops."

He spat viciously over the side and then called to his Percherons. Craig seated himself, watching the man go, wondering if Irish had not misgauged the sympathies of these farmers. He turned his face southward, knowing a moment's hesitation about going to Brockhalter's. The man was an ex-miner, known to sell MacQueen supplies from his store, and his wife was Garnet MacQueen's cousin. Then Craig shrugged it off, shaking out his reins. If the woman was sick, he had to see her.

Here and there out on Territory Road he passed fields of scrubby grain cleaved by the wide, dark swaths the harvesters had cut through them, leaving an acrid, dust-gray stubble to catch next winter's snow. It was a meager glimpse of the good years Craig had known here as a boy, with the dry, pungent scent of chaff and ripe grain titillating the nostrils like snuff, giving somber accent to the waste wrought by the silt on the rest of the land. Between these stretches of grain was nothing; the land lay fallow and hard and caked under the heat of midsummer.

Kootenai Cañon took the road through the foothills to the rock-ribbed shoulders of the Cabinets. Brockhalter's store was built in the shadow of these first real mountains upon the banks of the Fisher. It was a miserable log building with a low saddle roof, set in a grove of cottonwoods. To one side, in a stubble field, were the dismantled skeletons of old wagons, the ironwork leprous with brown rust. The yard before the door had been trampled hard and flat as cement through the years, with a sagging cottonwood tie rack planted beneath one window. A

105

settler's linchpin wagon was halted here, occupied by an enormously fat woman in soiled calico, holding a squalling baby on her lap. She watched the doctor suspiciously as he pulled his buckboard in, nodding to her before he stepped down.

He stood a moment beside his rig, eyes on the shadowed rectangle of the doorway, and the MacBell House rose vividly in his memory. He started to lift out his black bag, but it struck him that he would have no free hand if he did this. He left it in the buckboard and moved toward the building, not going directly into the door but approaching it at an angle, so that when he stopped before the opening, allowing his eyes to accustom themselves to the inner gloom, his body was not skylighted in the rectangle. The desultory talk from within ceased abruptly, and the two men at the counter turned to stare at Craig. He marked the lanky, overalled settler with a sad, weary face, standing before the counter, and the storekeeper behind it, short and square as a pig of Galena lead with a sullen, withdrawing look on his bearded face.

"Brockhalter?" he asked. "I'm Doctor Craig. I got word that your wife needed attention."

Brockhalter wiped slack, wet lips with the back of a hairy hand. "Whyntcha come on in?"

Craig stepped into the fruity offense of many odors, lying thick as syrup on the fetid air of the gloomy room. Dried apples mingled their tart piquancy with the cloying sweetness of blackstrap sorghum. The sour reek of forty-rod whiskey was so strong it touched Craig's mouth with the foul, cottony taste of a hangover. Brockhalter led him through this to a rear room that was filthier than the store with but one small window to ease the oppressive heat. The bed was a rude, pegged affair, filling half the chamber, tumbled with the faded patches of a homemade quilt and other soiled coverings.

Craig sighed heavily, defeatedly, and wondered how many

rooms like this he had walked into, how many more he would walk into before it was through. The woman was sallow and drawn, drenched with sweat, her hot, feverish body marked with the characteristic blotches.

"How long has she been this way?"

"About a week."

"Can you read?"

"Not very good, Doc."

"Then I'll tell you. I want her bathed, first of all, and clean bedding put on. I want that window screened. . . ."

"Ain't got any screen, Doc."

"Then a piece of muslin, anything to prevent insects getting in. That's important. . . ."

It was the same thing again, a weary catechism that he had repeated until he hardly gave the words a thought. Brockhalter stood there silently, scrubbing at his matted spade beard with thick, scarred fingers.

"What'll I do if she gets hungry?" he asked when Craig was through.

"Don't feed her," said Craig in exasperation. "Can't I get that through your head, Brockhalter? Nothing but milk mixed with lime water. Now, if you'll heat some water, I'll help you bathe her."

A dim flush filled the man's stolid face. "No man's goin' to put his hands on my wife nekkid."

Craig drew a heavy breath, clamping his teeth shut over his anger. "You bathe her, then," he said wearily. "But I want it done now so that I can check up. She's got to be clean, and she's got to be kept clean."

"I got customers to take care of."

"You mean you'd rather lose your wife than a few dollars?"

The sharp tone in Craig's voice snapped Brockhalter's head up. He stared at the doctor, his slack lips working faintly. Then he gave a final, vicious dig at his itching beard. "I'll have to go for water," he muttered.

"Get my bag from the buckboard while you're at it, will you?" Craig asked him. "I forgot it."

When Brockhalter had left, Craig moved out into the store, looking for a broom with which he could sweep the filthy room. The settler was gone, and the front chamber was empty. Craig saw a broom in a far corner and was walking toward it when a wagon entered the frame formed by the open door. It was coming down the road to the store, too far away at first to recognize the two people on the seat. But he could not mistake the rig itself. The cut-under front gear. The rack bed. The oversize brakes on the back wheels, so characteristic of a mountain wagon.

It filled him with a small, insidious suffocation, and he found the whole weight of his body changing, centering itself in the impulse to meet some opposing force. Then he saw that it was Washoe up on the seat with Garnet MacQueen beside him. His eyelids dropped in that hooded, studying way, until the flickering, livening little lights passing through his eyes were hardly visible. It gave his face a dangerous look.

He stepped to the door, taking careful account of all the small signs that could signify so much. Partridges were scratching in the grass covering the hummocks beyond the dooryard to his right, and, where these hummocks rose into the hillside itself, a long-tailed chat was squawking from one of the gnarled oaks. The gurgle of meager summer water came from the other direction, where the bottoms of the Fisher were hidden by a grove of cottonwoods. Brockhalter was supposed to be over there getting water, and his presence could have silenced what birds would normally be in the bottoms. Still, when Craig finally moved out, he put his own buckboard between himself and those bottoms and kept an ear out in the other direction, in case the chat or partridges should stop their sounds.

Garnet must have already recognized Pepper and Salt. Craig saw how uplifted with tension her body looked on the seat. When she saw him step out the door, she did not pull up. She drew her two-horse team to a halt just back of his buckboard, a fixed, strained expression filling her face as she stared at Craig.

"Come to butcher Missus Brockhalter?" she asked.

Craig felt his belly contract sickly, as if from a blow. "Garnet," he said, on a sudden impulse taking a step toward them.

Washoe's narrow, emaciated body lunged upward, as if to rise. Craig halted himself, and the cook did not complete the movement, remaining half risen, his legs braced against the toolbox that served for a footboard, his right hand gripping the sides of the seat. Craig's full attention was caught by the man then.

He realized how intently Washoe had been watching him from the first. That was natural. But the expression in the man's eyes wasn't. Craig looked in vain for the smoldering hatred that filled Garnet's eyes so turbulently. Washoe's eyes, now that Craig was meeting them directly, fluttered in an attempt to hold their gaze. Then they darted away, looking at the store without actually focusing on the building, coming back to Craig's with definite effort, only to lower to the ground.

"Doc," said Washoe, in a strained way, "Doc. . . ."

"Don't speak to him," Garnet told the cook. "Go in and get that flour from Brockhalter."

"Brockhalter's down at the river getting water," said Craig.

"Then go in and find what we need and have it on the counter by the time he comes back," Garnet told Washoe. The man stepped down off the wheel, stopping on the ground to cough softly for a moment. He took another strange look at Craig. There was something almost servile in the way his eyes shifted away. Then he shuffled into the store.

109

Craig turned back to Garnet, his good hand on the dusty iron tire of the wagon. For an instant he saw her attention flicker to his arm in the sling.

"Garnet," he said, "I've been wanting to speak with you. I can't tell you how badly I feel about Duncan."

"You must," she said acidly.

"Garnet, I've got to know. How did it happen?"

"With a hole some butcher cut in his stomach."

"No!" There was a tortured break to Craig's voice. "You know I don't mean that. There's got to be a reason. I was so sure I'd resected all of the gangrenous portion. He was so easy when I left him. Did he get restless again?"

"Not particularly."

"He would have, if infection had set in again. You could tell. He'd feel like he was on fire. Was it like that?"

"No. I don't want to talk about it. I. . . ."

"Please, Garnet. If he wasn't feverish, how did it happen?"

"Oh" — her head tossed in angry confusion — "I guess he was feverish. I don't know. He started thrashing around."

"When? How soon before he died?"

"Couple of hours, I guess."

"And he was quiet before that?"

"Will you stop it?"

"I can't. Don't you see, if he wasn't restless or feverish up to a couple of hours before his death, it couldn't have been infection. It wouldn't have killed him that quickly. What else could it be? Tell me everything that happened with Duncan after I left, everything you did. . . ."

"Damn you!" she muttered, and stepped off the wagon on the other side, walking down the team toward the store. He paralleled her on his side, reaching the heads of the horses at the same time she did.

"Leave me alone, Alan, I'm warning you."

110

He blocked her from going on. "Garnet, you've got to understand. You can't believe I'd do anything like that deliberately."

"Why not? You're Bob Craig's boy, aren't you?"

"That's what I mean," he said. "I know what they're saying in Coffin Gap. I know now why your dad didn't want me to touch Duncan up at the mine. He thought I'd come back in revenge for my dad's murder. But I didn't know that *then*. I didn't come back in revenge. I didn't want to believe those rumors about Jada's killing my dad when I first heard about them. I don't want to believe them now. Jada didn't kill my dad. That's all there is to it."

Those heavy brows were turned saffron in the fading afternoon light, twisting above her eyes into a deep frown. She could not help looking at his slinged arm again. "Even after what happened at the MacBell House?" she asked in a husky, reluctant way.

"Yes. I'm perfectly willing to forget that, if we can only straighten this out. All it will take is a mutual faith in each other, Garnet. If I have faith that Jada didn't kill my father, couldn't Jada believe that I didn't come back for revenge? What kind of doctor would I be, to take something like that out on an innocent kid? Do you honestly think I'm capable of it?"

For a moment the adamant lines of her face seemed to soften. Her parting lips held a damp, velvet texture. She shifted her whole head slightly, to look squarely up at him. Perhaps it was the change of light this brought into her eyes. It held an indefinable, sensual impact. He felt the blood thicken in his throat. He started to reach out for her, but, before he could, the whole expression was gone from her face, and she wheeled away, walking swiftly back to the wagon.

"Garnet," he followed her, breathing huskily, "you've got to believe me."

She halted, faced into the wagon, with her back to him. A last, fading shaft of the sun slanted through the cottonwoods, picking out the curves of her body with its highlight and shadow till they held all the luscious nubility of ripened fruit.

"You make it hard, Alan. Part of me wants to believe you. But there are so many things I can't overlook, so many things I didn't see at first."

"What things?" he said, standing so close now the warmth of her body reached him. She did not speak, but her head was turned enough so that her profile was visible, and he could not miss the momentary drop of her attention to the bulge his Remington made beneath his coat. "My gun?" he asked, not understanding yet. "What's that got to do with it? You were the very one who asked me to take it that first time."

"I know, I know," she said miserably. "And it seemed perfectly natural, then. When I remembered who you really were, and how Bowie had taught you, it seemed natural. But. . . ."

"You mean a doctor who was capable of using a gun on somebody would be just as capable of killing them by other means," he said, understanding her now, forcing his words out in a harsh brutality.

"Oh, no."

"Yes!" he said. "Why not be plain? Capable of killing Duncan in revenge. That's what's in your mind." He was silent for a moment, staring at little burning auburn lights in her hair. "Did it ever strike you that a gun can save a life as well as take it?"

She turned her head to send a sharp, hot glance at him. "What are you talking about?"

"About Ingo Hubbard and Evan Fox," said Craig. "If I hadn't worn my gun that day, they would have stopped us from going up the mountain. If I hadn't seen your brother, he would

112

have died that day, Garnet. It did save his life for that day, anyway."

"I don't see what. . . ."

"And by the same token a surgeon's scalpel can take a life as well as save it. I've seen it happen. Just one mistake, one little wrong movement down there inside a man, and it's all over. Should the surgeon discard his scalpel then?"

"Oh, now you're just trying to confuse me. . . ."

"I don't think you're confused at all. I'm just trying to show you that a scalpel has no more bad or good in it than a gun. Only what men put there. I wouldn't wear this gun if I didn't have to. But you were the first to ask me to wear it. I couldn't have gotten beyond Ingo and Evan without it. I couldn't have stopped your father, up on the mountain. I used to try and reconcile it myself. A gun just didn't seem to have any place in a doctor's life. But what Bowie told me before I left had enough truth in it to make me keep the gun. He said a man didn't discard a skill so easily that he had taken so long to acquire. He said I wouldn't forget it, and the people out here wouldn't forget it. I think the past few weeks have proven that. Theoretically, it can't be reconciled. But a man can't live on theory out here. Why try to reconcile it? It's a fact. I'd be a fool not to face it. We live in a place where a doctor has to wear a gun, just the same as everybody else, and he ought to be damn' glad he's as good with it as he is."

"Oh, stop it, Alan, stop it!"

"All right," he said. "I don't think you really care much about that anyway. If you really were convinced that I butchered Duncan, you wouldn't have to drag the gun in as an extra reason for hating me."

"Alan . . . I. . . ."

The turning motion of her body, as she said it, brought her deep, soft breast up against his chest. She stopped there, lips parted, without any words coming out. Doubt stirred shadows deeply in her eyes. It lasted for an instant, with the two of them staring at each other. Craig could almost see the primal, animal attraction vibrating between them. He had the giddy sense of hovering on some sharp brink, with an immense, irresistible force pushing at him from behind. Then the whole thing dissolved, and he swung his broken arm out of the way, moving in hard against her until she was pressed tightly against the wagon. The ripeness of her body strained against him with the impulse to fight it. He met that with his own body and with his lips.

For a moment the fight seemed suspended in her. Then she was struggling again. She wedged one arm between them and levered him away. Ribs swelling with the panting breath passing through them, she stared at him with the blank eyes of an enraged cat. Without warning, she tore the buggy whip from its socket and lashed it viciously across his face. He stumbled backward, blinded by the pain, with her voice breaking against him as vitriolic, as biting as the whip.

"Not that way, either, you butcher. I still think you murdered my brother. Now, get away, get out, before I kill you!"

Chapter Nine

The bottom of Kootenai Cañon was drowned in shadow when Craig reached it on his way back from Brockhalter's. The tops of the cliffs, however, were still burnished by the dying touch of the sun. A marmot whistled from somewhere up there. It held a lonely sound. It only accented the discouragement in Craig.

It had been anger when he first left Garnet, to go back in the store. That had faded to a rankling bitterness as he occupied himself with Mrs. Brockhalter. When her husband came back with the water, Craig made no attempt to explain the bloody whip stripe on his face, but he could see the man make his own mocking judgment of it. When Craig finally left the store, Garnet and the mountain wagon were gone. The bitterness had fled him by then, leaving only a deep sense of failure as oppressive as the defeat he had first known on hearing of Duncan's death. It did not allow him to take much account of the road, as he free-bitted his team into Kootenai Cañon. But the chill of the shadows lifted him from this mood, causing him to shiver in his coat and look around a little.

This cañon headed almost due north toward Coffin Gap, with the Fisher running through its bottom. Territory Road hugged the west wall almost to the end, then crossed the river on Fisher Bridge, to finish out the cañon along its east wall. The walls themselves reeled above the rattling buckboard in great, tiered escarpments, drawing so close together at times that the strip of sky at the top looked no wider than a rifle barrel, sloping out at other points to evoke tributary cañons that passed quickly back into the cliffs, as if disappearing on some mysterious, Pleistocene errand.

Craig was still looking about him when he passed the mouth of one of these cañons. The earth here was ruffled with fresh hoofmarks, and he slowed down to read them. It was clear sign of a big cut of cattle being driven to higher summer pastures, probably Coronet beef. But why had they turned off into that spur cañon when it would have been so much easier to push on through the Kootenai? He stared in vague disturbance up the narrow, tortured gorge of that spur. There was no sound, but he caught sight of a dim haze of dust that seemed to be rising from the gorge and settling against the sky.

Craig drove on, frowning at the bridge as it came into view ahead. The marmot whistled again, far behind him now, and the echoes turned the rocks to hooting gargoyles. Bit chains rattled nervously with the fretting toss of Pepper's head.

"Heah, gal," Craig called throatily to the black mare, in an effort to quiet her. He didn't want any trouble while he had to hold the reins with just one hand. But somehow the horses had transmitted their nervousness to him. Faint, crinkling lines formed about his squinted eyes as he stared up at the scowling walls. The evergreens at the top looked almost black, and the rusty outcroppings had taken on a dark, bloody hue.

Again the chill of the shadows seemed to bite at him, and he shrugged impatiently in his coat, shaking the reins slightly to speed up the trotting animals. Black rump and white rump moved in smooth unison. Wheels rattled and bolsters popped as the wagon gained speed. For a moment Craig lost his spookiness in watching the impeccable teamwork of the animals he loved so well. Their flanks were rippling silk. Their manes were flaunted banners. Then, Pepper whinnied shrilly and tossed her head once more.

The direction of that toss, more than anything, brought Craig's own head up. Some indistinct, flickering motion high on the fissured wall of the cañon drew his attention. A hawk left its perch up there and started a swooping drop downward. It veered away from the wall, suddenly, wings working violently as it strove to rise back. Craig squinted his eyes more tightly in an effort to see what had startled the bird. Then he lowered his attention angrily to the road.

What the hell's the matter? I'm tired again, that's all. That scene with Garnet just made me jumpy. If I don't. . . .

The shot came like a giant handclap.

Craig was almost pitched back off the seat as the horses bolted. His grip on the reins was the only thing that saved him. This pulled the horses' heads up violently. The pain only filled them with further panic. Even in that instant, fighting to center his balance, he saw the fresh, white wood chipped off the boards where the bullet had struck the seat six inches from his hip.

"Whoa, Pepper," he shouted, "whoa, Salt, settle down there, girls, whoa."

But they were racing down the narrow, treacherous road at a frenzied, break-neck pace, and he was unable to bring them in hand. His whole body grew rigid with an almost uncontrollable impulse to jump. But he could not leave the horses that way, sure they would run themselves off the edge on one of those hairpins beyond.

"Hey, there, easy, now, easy."

Coat whipped out behind him, shirt plastered against the bony planes of his chest and ribs, he leaned forward, gathering the reins into his one good hand, and started a steady, hard series of jerks. He felt that Salt had the bit in her mouth, but the jerking dislodged it, put the bar up where it belonged. For a moment he felt himself gaining control over the beasts. Then another shot crashed.

This time Pepper lurched in her run and seemed to leap upward. She caught up the headlong gallop again and ran for a moment. He knew she was wounded, and his efforts to slow them down became more desperate.

"Whoa, there, girls. Hey, Pepper, you're pulling us off, hey, there, girl."

She had begun to veer and wobble badly, tugging Salt over against her. Still going at that breakneck pace, this slued the back end of the wagon around against the cliff on the right side. There was a rending crash, a clatter of broken wheels. It did not diminish their speed. With a frenetic scream, the white mare lunged on forward, pulling the lurching, stumbling black horse with her.

The smashed wheels at the rear slued across the road in the other direction, toward the shoulder that dropped off into the river. Craig gave one last effort at straightening the animals out. Then he realized that it was impossible to control them one-handed. The whole rig was going, so he dropped the reins and rolled out.

He had taken enough falls to hit limp. He flopped down the ditch like a tumbleweed, gasping with the pain of rocks and sun-baked earth smashing at him. He heard the clattering, roaring passage of the wagon as it was pulled on down the road by those frenzied animals. As he came to a violent stop at the bottom, all piled up in a heap, he had a last, dazed view of the rig. It was still crashing down the road, tilted at a forty-five degree angle on the edge. Pepper stumbled and went off at the same instant that the smashed rear wheel pulled the wagon over. The whole outfit did a somersault in midair, landing halfway down the slope, and crashing on to the riverbank.

Dust settled like a pall, delicately, somberly over the carnage. There was no movement from the horses. *Killed, then,* thought Craig, and felt a hot adrenal flood of anger. He crawled from the mucky, summer shallows of the river, wincing at the stabs of pain from his bad arm, wondering if it were broken again. He reached a deep fissure in the slope and crouched, partly protected, staring up at the cliff across the road. He saw that movement again up there. The anger swelled in him once more, thickening his throat.

All the bright, searching little reflections normally livening his eyes were gone. The light seemed to lose itself down some dark shaft of him into the very depths, catching a smoky, primitive turbulence that had nothing to do with the civilization that had spawned and shaped the man. The marmot no longer whistled. The hawk was not in sight. The silence held pregnant weight.

Sprawled there in the fissure, he realized that, though he was protected from some portions of the cliff, there were high spots that would still reveal him to anyone gaining them. It caused him to crawl down toward the bridge.

It was a painful, dusty passage, taking advantage of what meager cover there was, jumpy with the tension of waiting for the next shot from above him. He could see movement and flashes of light on gun metal. Sometimes it looked higher, sometimes lower. He could not guess what they were doing. Then it disappeared completely, and he could no longer see any sign. He crawled past the dead animals, pinned beneath the smashed rig, lying in a gruesome heap in the shallow water. The dark, frightening things rose nearer the surface of his eyes.

He reached the bridge finally. The brackish water running in the bottom of the ditch, deepened here to a green, mucky pool, was edged with the bronzed, sickly gold of diseased dodder. There was no telling how deep it was, and he did not want to wade into it. But he was still too exposed here from above. The only way to gain the protection of the bridge was to climb up under the trestles. He slipped his gun away and reached up with his one good hand for the first rough, scaly timber. It was difficult with only one arm. He slipped off the first time, tearing his coat and almost pitching into the coppery pool. Finally he got up on the first level and started to move underneath the main section.

The timbers were nothing more than undressed logs with the bark still on, and they had become so slippery with moss during the high water of winter and spring that Craig could not have kept his footing without the help of his good hand. Frogs croaked sleepily from the other end of the pool. The lazy peace of the sound formed a macabre contrast to the savage tension filling him. It was cold in the dark shadows. Drying sweat formed a crusty edge about his lips.

Then the frogs stopped.

Craig arrested all movement. He stared in a stiff, peering way through the shadowy pattern of trestles. Had his presence caused that? No. Cousin Jack's had.

The man appeared at the opposite end of the bridge. His gun was holstered, too, so he could use both hands to hold on. An upright support had hidden him from view until now. He stepped from behind it, and the two men saw each other in the same instant. Jack's great sloth-like eyes shone viscid as jelly in the dim light.

Craig had that one moment to see how it was. When Jack went for his gun, he would still have one hand left on the overhead support to keep him from falling. When Craig went for his, he would have no hands, and he knew the movement of his draw would make him lose his footing. He would have to let go completely then, not mar his aim by fighting it, and hope for one clear shot as he fell. As this decision formed itself in Craig's mind, Cousin Jack's eerie eyes blinked once, and he let go with his right hand.

Craig's feet started slipping off the log the moment he released his hold. He relaxed completely, slapping for his gun. He was falling backward as he fired.

Cousin Jack had not yet gotten his gun free when his body jerked with Craig's bullet. The man doubled over, left arm pawing blindly at thin air, and he followed Craig down.

Craig fell without striking any timbers. He held his gun above his head, hoping to keep it dry. But the water was over his head and over the gun, held up as it was. He struck bottom and rolled over. He half crawled, half swam along the muddy bottom to a depth where his head was above the surface. Cousin Jack lay on his stomach with his head submerged in the water. Craig found footing beneath him and floundered over in that direction. He was still up to his waist when something caused him to turn part way around.

Jada MacQueen appeared through the trestles, coming toward the bridge from the same side as Craig had. In violent instinct Craig lifted his gun. The movement caught MacQueen's attention, and he tried to get his own gun in line. Craig's trigger was already jumping softly beneath his pulling finger. And the hammer made a dark, metallic click against the wet brass of a cartridge too dampened with water to fire. Craig squeezed the trigger again in a wild, desperate way. Once more that damp, impotent clank of metal on metal. And MacQueen's over-and-under gun was leveled on Craig.

The shot was multiplied to a weird, ear-splitting volley by the echoes, billowing up and down the cañon in a great, roaring surf of sound. Craig's whole body jerked with reaction. But there was no pain.

He stared incredulously at MacQueen, only then realizing that the shot had not come from the over-and-under. MacQueen's legs were already going out from under him, and there was a foolish, blank look on his face. His gun went off, but it was pointed at the bridge near him, driving the bullet up through the mossy flooring.

He fell into a sitting position, sliding down almost to the

water, where he stopped. He made some effort to pull his rifle around once more.

"Throw it in the river, Jada."

It was Bowie French's voice, coming from the bridge above. MacQueen stared upward at something Craig could not see. His great chest stirred with a heavy, angry breath. Then he shoved the rifle off into the slimy water. The bridge trembled faintly to the clip-clop of a horse's hoofs. Bowie French came into view, riding off the end of the bridge onto the road. He still had his Paterson in his hand, and the sharp, droll smile Craig remembered so well curled his lips.

"I was helping push some beef into higher pastures," he said, stepping down off his pied horse. "Up in the rimrock when I heard the shots. Came back along the edge, Alan, and saw how they were pinching you down here. Thought you might appreciate a little help."

"I do, Bowie. And thanks." He was trembling now, in reaction. He glanced at MacQueen, realizing how close he had been to death. Then that faded, as he slopped out of the muck. He crouched over Cousin Jack long enough to see that he was dead, and made his way over to MacQueen, with Bowie coming along behind. He lowered himself by the big, red-headed miner and reached out for the wounded leg. MacQueen pulled back with a jerk.

"Lemme alone. If you're going to kill me, get it over with."

Craig lifted his head to stare at the man. "Nobody's going to kill you, Jada."

"Oh, now, Alan, boy," said Bowie sardonically from behind Craig. It caused the doctor to turn part way about. Bowie stood with his gun out yet, a mocking expression on his face. "Jada's tried to kill you twice. Let him go and he'll just try it again."

"What do you propose?"

"What do you think?"

"That would be murder, Bowie."

"If you haven't got the sand, I'll be glad to oblige."

Craig gazed at Bowie with something dying in him. The man was still smiling, but his eyes held no humor, no depth of expression at all, only blank, shimmering surfaces, like shiny, soulless buttons.

"Put the gun away, Bowie," he said wearily. "I'm going to fix his leg." He reached for MacQueen's leg once more, and MacQueen pulled away again. Craig raised his eyes to the man impatiently. "You're bleeding like a stuck pig. If it's a severed artery, you won't last long without help."

"Think I'd let you touch me, after what you did to him?" asked MacQueen in a guttural, muttering way. His eyes were on Cousin Jack now, and he seemed to lose awareness of Craig or Bowie. His lips barely moved as he spoke, and his ugly, scarred face was warped strangely. "Best lode miner in the States. Stuck by me when everybody else turned tail. Even my daughter turned on me, bringing you up there to kill Duncan, bringing a *Craig*. Jack was the only one that stuck. All the way through. Only Jack. Got me out of that cave-in when I was coyoting at Virginia City, didn't he? Nobody else'd go down the drift. It was going to slip farther, and they knew it. So here comes Jack. And when that gas broke loose in the Jada Hole. I would have been killed. He come then, didn't he? Only Jack. Come all that way beside me and then gets cut down by some butcher in fancy pants who calls himself a doctor. . . ."

The stubborn blindness of it finally struck anger in Craig, and he checked it with difficulty. "Listen, Jada," he said thinly, "don't be a fool. Let me fix that leg."

"Don't touch me," snarled MacQueen. He began dragging himself up the bank of the pool, slowly, painfully. "I'll get you for this. I'll get you, Craig. I won't eat, but what I'll see Jack's empty chair beside me. I won't sleep, but what I'll dream of

123

Duncan. I won't quit till I get you now. You won't have no hospital. Count on that. If I don't get you before then, you won't have no hospital, you won't have nothing. . . ."

Craig made no further movement, watching the man drag himself up the mucky side of the pool, leaving a trail of viscid blood behind till he was at the lip of the gully, pulling himself over to disappear. It was only then that Craig realized that Bowie was watching him instead of MacQueen. He turned to see a quizzical, wondering light in Bowie's eyes.

"You really got that doctor idea bad, haven't you? I guess I really didn't understand . . . till now. A man tries to kill you, and you turn around and want to fix his wound for him."

"Why didn't you kill him with that first shot, if you want him dead so badly?" Craig asked in exasperation.

"All I could see was his legs from where I was on the bridge," Bowie replied mildly. "He slid down out of sight before I could get a second bean out of my wheel. When I got down here, you was in my way."

"If I hadn't been here, would you have shot him again when you came down?"

"Maybe."

"Because there wouldn't have been a witness to see you do murder?"

"Don't shoulder me now, Alan."

"You could have shot me, too. Then there wouldn't have been a witness. What's the difference . . . one murder or two?"

"Dammit, cut it out. You know I wouldn't think of that with you."

"What were you thinking of the last time we met, when you asked me to leave the room before you did something?"

"I was snaky. I wasn't my natural self. Now I am, Alan. We're together, the way we used to be. There's every reason why we should be. There's nothing else left for you. MacQueen

124

must have convinced you of that by now. He's tried to wreck you at every turn. He's smashed your rig, killed the horses you put so much pride in, tried to kill you twice. You're in our wagon for good now."

Craig gazed somberly at Bowie, seeing the humor in the lean, weathered face, the warm, kindling lights that could come into those eyes. He knew that he was looking — as much as was possible — at what he had known of the man before. It brought a momentary warmth to their old friendship, a friendship Bowie was offering him now, probably for the last time. There was a painful reluctance in Craig to mar this moment. Yet he had to say what was in him.

"I'm still a doctor."

Bowie gazed at Craig for such a long space the doctor thought he did not mean to answer. Then that droll curl of Bowie's lips, so near a smile, faded. The great, arched box of his ribs swelled against his shirt.

"And if MacQueen sent you another call from up there on the mountain, you'd go running?"

"I guess I would."

This brought Bowie forward, his whole body gripped in a tension more savage than Craig had ever seen in him before. The doctor wondered what tenuous thread held the man from lashing out. When Bowie finally spoke, it was so low, and so guttural, Craig could hardly hear it. Each word tred slowly forward, trembling with a restraint so intense it held pain.

"Alan, you're a damned fool. And I'm a damned fool for saving your life. I won't do it again. From here on out, you and I are on opposite sides of the street. And, by God, you'd better not let me catch you on my side when I come to town!"

Chapter Ten

The rest of the summer was not measured in days. It was a febrile, crawling thing, divided into a succession of moaning, delirious, vomiting patients who stirred restlessly beneath the tumbled covers of beds standing in stinking, unscreened rooms. Craig would not have believed a human being could exist on so little sleep. Some days he went twenty-four hours without seeing his own bed. He dozed in the saddle, or caught an hour's nap during a lonely vigil while waiting for some crisis to pass. He only got to his room every two or three days. Each day he thought the peak of the epidemic had passed, and each day it grew.

Craig lost weight and appetite. He wore his clothes too long without changing and developed a rash of which he could not rid himself. He didn't remove his shoes often enough, and his feet swelled up so that Irish had to cut the shoes away.

And then there was MacQueen, hovering about the rim of Craig's every thought, his every activity, like a mordant ghoul waiting to exact its toll. The man had been seen at Brockhalter's, or sighted by one of the cattlemen up in the Cabinets, or seen on the outskirts of town. Craig was too stupefied for the most part to take heed, or to care. He had reached the point at which he thought he could go on no longer when something happened that gave him new hope. He came downstairs one morning to find Irish and Asa Gardener alone in the saloon, toasting to the new hospital.

"I'm on my way to Keeler for the lumber, Doc," Gardener told him. "None of those undressed logs for your walls now. Whipsawed lumber and finished siding. Tongue-in-groove flooring, three feet off the ground. No damn' puncheon Davy Crockett logs with enough space between them for a small bear to crawl through. Screening and plumbing and sinks and bath-tubs. . . ."

"Where did you get the money?" broke in Craig. "Last count, we didn't have nearly enough."

"We got it," grinned Irish.

"You didn't dig into your bank account," Craig accused him.

"What bank account?" You know I'm broke."

"The saloon, then. You didn't mortgage it?"

"Already got two mortgages on it. Nobody'd take a third. Don't worry about the money, Alan. It's there. We didn't hold up any banks to get it. You'll have your hospital."

Craig turned dubiously to Asa. "You know the risk you're taking?"

"After what you did for my wife, this is small potatoes. I'll be all right. We've sent the money ahead by bank draft. I'm taking a horse down to the Absaroka Crossing way station, picking up the stage there. By the time Bowie finds out what's going on, I'll be on my way back with the lumber and a double crew of the toughest teamsters in Keeler. If Coronet wants to jump me then, just let 'em."

So Asa Gardener left, and Craig dug deeper into the grim, tenacious forces of himself to hold on till the man got back. He was riding horseback, now, not wanting to trust himself to a wagon again after that experience in Kootenai Cañon, taking little used roads to his patients and traveling the ridges whenever he could, so it would be him looking down upon whatever lay below, instead of somebody else looking down on him. He got as spooky and suspicious as a high-liner and automatically pulled the skirt of his coat back whenever he approached a building.

On the eighth day after Gardener had left for Keeler, the horse Craig had been using developed a limp, and he had to return to Fields's Livery for another animal. He was sitting in a stupor on a bench, just within the barn door, waiting for the hosteler to saddle up for him, when another man came in. The man said something. Craig thought he was talking to Fields. Then he felt the man shove his shoulder.

"Do you hear me, Alan?"

"Huh?" asked Craig stupidly.

"I said Asa's on the way back with the lumber." It was Irish. "He wrote a letter last Tuesday, but the stage didn't get it here till today. That means he's over half way back to Coffin Gap. Are you listening?"

"Sure," said Craig. "That's fine."

"You aren't going out again?"

"Missus Ward's in labor pains up at Brockhalter's."

"I thought that was Missus Ward's baby you delivered yesterday, Doc?" said Fields.

"Was it?" Craig peered stupidly around. "Well, maybe."

"You can't go out, Alan," Irish told him. "You haven't eaten today. You haven't slept, to my knowledge, since that nap yesterday morning you took in the saloon. Listen, man. . . ."

"I gotta go," said Craig thickly, drunkenly. "Somebody called for me. Who'd you say it was, Harry?"

"That dirt farmer out on Bucket Creek. His kid's got the typhoid."

"Oh, sure. Gambel."

"Not Gambel. That was Gambel in the Flats this morning. Fitzsimmons."

"Sure. Fitzsimmons."

"Fitzsimmons, hell," said Irish. "If he wants his kid tended, he can bring him in. You just can't go any more."

"I've got to." Craig rose with a vague, flailing motion of his arms, groping his way to the horse. "I'll be all right. Sleep on the horse."

"And fall off and break your neck. You're not going, Alan."

"Got to." *Who was hanging on him like that?* "Leggo, Irish." *Shove at them. That was it. Shove at them.* He shoved at them. They stopped hanging. He lifted his foot for the stirrup. *Where was it? Where are you?* Someone was grabbing at him again. "Got to. Leggo. Gotta go."

"Not this time, Alan. I'm sorry."

What for, Gabriel? Craig was spun around. Then he knew what for. It made a sharp, cracking sound somewhere way up in his head. It did not knock him clear out. He felt himself sag into Irish's arms tiredly, almost gratefully. There was the mutter of voices. Then someone lifted his feet off the ground. There was no pain. It was almost funny. Time contracted and expanded. It was a minute till he felt the bed beneath him. A year. He didn't know which. He didn't care. He was floating off to some warm lotus land, feeling the somnolent, drunken smile tilt his lips. What paradise sleep was. He stood outside its door for that last moment, savoring it, then stepped in. . . .

When he awoke, it was daylight. He lay in bed, luxuriating in the drowsy warmth of the room. He began to listen intently for sounds from the saloon below, trying to tell what time it was. There was no noise. It must be morning, then. He had slept through since yesterday afternoon.

He took a heavy, sighing breath, gazing around the room. The jade Buddha. The guayacon. The straw-quilted wine bottle. It struck Craig how often he had awakened in this room, surrounded by the things of Gabriel Irish's so few people really knew about. It filled him with a nostalgic sadness. The mood was still with him when Irish tapped softly on the door and peeked around its edge. When he saw that Craig was awake, he stepped in.

"I won't apologize for the sock," he grinned.

Craig answered it with his own smile. "Next time I'll duck."

Irish sat on the bed, slipping a pair of Craig's slim cigars from the pocket of the doctor's coat where it hung on the chair. He thrust one between Craig's teeth and lit it, then occupied himself with his own. When he had it going, he waved out the match, speaking between the strong, white teeth clamped around the cigar.

"There's water heating for your tub, breakfast waiting whenever you want it. Gentleman George is getting clean clothes from your room. Anything else?"

Craig lay back, hands behind his head, taking a long drag before he spoke. "Yes, Gabriel. Why do you do all this for me?"

The other man removed his cigar, studying it. "I should be offended," he said.

"No," protested Craig. "We've let it go without asking for long enough now. We've just sort of slipped into it, without questioning, until I'm practically boarding in your place, until you're everything from my business manager to my personal valet. You've incurred the antagonism of the cattlemen by it, the most powerful interests in the basin. It isn't only your business you're risking. It means a threat to your person. Not that I don't feel grateful, or that I could have done much without your help. I'd just like to know."

Irish stood and walked to the window, opening it wide to lean on the sill and stare out across the rooftops, leading off toward the somber, brooding mountains.

"My friendship with your father had a lot to do with it in the beginning," he said at last. "But that ceased to be the cause of it very soon. You'd stand on your own two feet in any crowd, Alan." He paused, studying the cigar as he twirled it between his fingers. "Maybe it's because you're the only man in this whole town with guts enough to use his intelligence and stay neutral in this fight between the valley men and MacQueen."

"I didn't think the issue meant that much to you."

Irish shrugged. "Maybe not the issue itself. But it brings out what a man is. Did it ever strike you that someone who belongs to neither side is riding a lonely trail?"

"I went into it with my eyes open. It isn't only this fight that sets me apart. In a town like this my profession would do that anyway."

"I know what you mean," Irish murmured. "You see people all day long, talk with them, joke with them, probably know more about their business, their lives, than their own family. Yet how many of them do you really get close to? A man can be as lonely in a crowd as in a desolation, sometimes."

Craig gazed at the man, struck by how close it came to how he had felt so many times. It filled him with that same sense of revelation he had known before, when Irish had told him of the *caraba*, and they had talked this way. Only now it was not tantalizing; it was not incomplete. He realized he was being given a glimpse of the man few people had obtained — a glimpse of loneliness so deep it startled him, all the more poignant for its contrast to the surface picture of suave, genial urbanity Irish always imparted downstairs.

"Are you drawing a parallel, Gabriel?" he asked. "A man doesn't know that much about loneliness unless he's experienced it."

"Maybe."

"Nobody would have guessed it."

"They're not supposed to," answered Irish. "You've got to be one of the boys in this business. I grin like a Cheshire, pass along the thoughts of the great on drinking, send everybody home potted and happy. You've got to make compromises in life, no matter what you do. Those are mine. It doesn't bother me much, most of the time. But when somebody like you comes along, who understands what . . . ah. . . ." He broke off in

131

disgust, waving it away, as he turned to Craig. "Why talk about it? Why not just sum it up with a drink from the *caraba?* Will you join me?"

Craig looked at him for a long time without answering, allowing the full ramifications of the offer to fill him. Then he nodded. "I'd be honored, Gabriel."

Irish was reaching for the Persian bottle when the stairs shook, then the hall outside creaked, and Gentleman George appeared in the door. "Boss, you better come right down. There's a rider here from the wagon train with bad news."

Irish glanced at Craig, face darkening. "He means Asa's lumber train. You'd better come down, too."

Craig slipped into his pants and shoes, and twisted into a shirt on the way down. The rider was near the front door in a small crowd of house men. He was grimy, hollow-eyed, his jeans marbled with the dirty, drying lather of a hard-ridden horse.

"What's the trouble?" Irish asked him.

"We was attacked last night, about thirty-five miles south of here," the man told them. "Wasn't Indians, because they all had guns, and we didn't hear a whoop among them. We managed to drive them off. They wrecked a couple of wagons and killed a driver. One of the wagons went off the road onto a talus bank and pinned a man beneath it. The front wheel crumbled and laid the wagon bed right down on his leg. The whole outfit is hung up on a rock, but we can't touch it for fear it will slide on down the talus bank and crush him completely. The most we could do was sling ropes around it and hope it will hold till somebody gets there. You were the nearest doctor."

"How can a doctor help, if they can't get the wagon off him?" Craig asked.

"Like I say, the man's leg is the part of him pinned," said

the rider. "If the leg could be cut off without upsetting the wagon, he'd be free."

"Is he one of your drivers?" Irish asked.

"No," the man told them. "He's one of the bunch that jumped us. Said his name was Evan Fox . . . from Coronet."

Irish insisted on going with Craig. It would have shaved an hour and a half off their traveling time to go by horseback, but they both agreed that kind of ride would so weary Craig he would be in very poor shape to operate. The Missoula stage was due out in half an hour, and Irish got two tickets on it. The driver knew what was up and pushed his teams far past their usual eight-mile-an-hour average. It was thirty-five miles to Hellgate Junction, and they made it in less than three hours. From there it was only a couple of miles farther south to where the wagons were.

It was a strange, subdued scene. The late afternoon shadows crawled across the line of immense, dead-axle lumber wagons piled up at the side of the road, their mule teams standing restlessly in harness, stiff and briny with dried sweat. There must have been more than two dozen teamsters gathered at the end of the train, on the shoulder of the road. A couple of fires had been lighted, and some of them were drinking coffee from rusty tin cups. Asa Gardener himself was at the stage door when it stopped, helping Craig out. His primitive, sweating face revealed the strain the responsibility of the last two weeks had caused him. A marked loss of weight was evident in vague, shadowy hollows that hovered beneath his Neanderthal cheekbones. His eyes were bloodshot and red-rimmed, and he kept rubbing them with his fists.

"I'm sure glad you came, Doc," he muttered. "I ain't never run into anything like this before. I didn't know what to do. Some of the boys was for pushing the wagon on over and letting it crush him. I almost had to fight them over it. He killed the

133

wagon master's cousin, you know."

As he was talking, Asa led them through the grumbling, nervous crowd of teamsters to the edge of the drop off. It was a steep talus slope, falling a hundred feet into a deep gorge before it reached any timber. The wagon had gone clear off the edge to be stopped about half way down by an immense boulder. It hung there precariously, tilted over on one side and toward the front. Craig could see two dead mules where they had slid down from the wagon, clear into the timber at the bottom of the slope. A third hung in its harness from the wagon tongue.

"We had to shoot that one," said Asa.

"Ought to do the same with that damn' cowpoke," growled a big, bearded man with a wad of tobacco in one cheek so immense it looked as if the jaw was disjointed.

"You the wagon master?" Craig asked him.

"Dick Joliet," offered Asa.

"I notice you've got ropes hitched on," Craig told Joliet. "Why couldn't you put a team on each end and pull the wagon up just enough to get him out from underneath?"

"That was our idea," said Joliet. The tobacco gave his voice a juicy sound. "But, when we started to pull, the wagon began to slide. I don't think the lines we have are heavy enough to hold the outfit anyway. One of them snapped when it started going. It's so tricky we was even afraid some movement of the teams might upset it, so we unhitched them and made the ropes fast to our wagons up here. It's the most we can do, Doc. That talus slides so much a man takes his life in his hands going down on a rope. Asa tried it and almost upset the outfit on himself. The slightest touch and she moves."

"Can you see Fox from any point up here?"

"No. He's right down under her. He's still conscious, though. We lowered some coffee down to him about half an

134

hour ago, and the cup came back up empty."

Craig's lips were thin as he glanced at Irish. Then he looked down again at the wagon. "If you'll rig up a rope for me, I'll go down."

Joliet tucked horny, scarred thumbs into his greasy galluses, teetering back on his heels. "I don't know as I want to take the responsibility for this, Doc. I don't think you can do it without upsetting that wagon on yourself."

Craig turned to the man. "Are you thinking about me as much as you are about your cousin?"

Joliet studied Craig from eyes that held a withdrawn light, stirred dimly by the turgid, slowly resolved things moving in his mind. He turned aside to spit.

"It would be hard to tell you how I felt about my cousin, Doc," he said. "We'd worked together with this freighting line for about fifteen years. I only wish that cowhand was up here, on his two legs, and I could get my hands on him for a little while."

"And I'd be the first to step aside and let you at him," said Craig. "But this is different, Joliet. You've been driving mules a long time, haven't you?"

A curious surprise slackened Joliet's jaw. A yellow streak of tobacco juice escaped his parted lips to dribble down into his beard. He wiped irritably at this.

"I been whackin' their hides most of my life. What's that got to do with it?"

"Did you ever stop to think what a thin line separates a man from a mule?"

Joliet removed his hands from his galluses, the ponderous, muscular weight of his body coming forward off his heels.

"Dick . . . ," began Asa.

"Shut up, Asa," growled the wagon boss. His eyes tightened to a mean, little squint as he bent toward Craig. "It ain't many

135

men with the brass to call me a jackass, Doctor."

"I'm not calling you one, Joliet. The choice really lies with yourself."

Joliet stared sullenly at Craig with those small, turgid lights changing slowly in his eyes. For a moment the doctor thought it had made no impression on him. Then, as slowly and ponderously as a load of lumber shifting in one of his own wagons, the man's weight teetered back onto his heels once more. He reached up to hook his thumbs back in his suspenders, emitting a rueful snort.

"I guess you're right, Doc. A man don't get many chances to prove his difference from an animal, does he? I'll have the boys rig you up a sling to lower you down."

"Two slings," put in Irish. Craig started to protest, but Irish waved it away. "You'll need somebody to hand you things if you're going to operate. Don't argue with me now. Hasn't the man been down there long enough?"

Craig shrugged helplessly, thanks in his eyes, and then turned to supervise the anchoring of the ropes. The ropes tied to the wagon down there were anchored to an outfit directly above it on the road. Craig had the men anchor the slings they were going to use to the next outfit in line. Dropping straight down from here, they would reach the level of the wrecked wagon about fifteen feet to its right. That way, when they moved over to the wagon, the ropes holding them would be slanting in at an angle from above. If they had to get out quickly, they could cast loose, and their own weight would carry them in a pendulum motion across the steep face of the slope away from the wagon, until their ropes reached the vertical again. Finally, Craig asked Joliet if there was a knot they could tie into the sling that would hold them securely and yet come loose in case the rope got snagged.

"Sheepshank might do it," offered the wagon boss. "It'll

hold as long as there's any tension against it. If you get the rope snagged under the wagon down there and can't swing free, all you got to do is give slack between you and the knot, and she'll come apart. We'll keep tension on the rope from up here all the time, unless you yell. That do it?"

"Sounds like it. All set, Gabriel?"

"All set."

The muleskinners lined up on the ropes like tug-of-war teams, making a sweating, grunting, cursing struggle of lowering the two men over the edge. That faded above Craig as he passed on down. The shale was too deep and slippery to keep their feet, and within a short space both Craig and Irish were sprawled against the face of the slope on their bellies, fighting to hold back the small avalanches each movement started. It took them fifteen minutes of painful, treacherous labor to reach the level of the wagon. They halted here a moment before starting the horizontal movement across the slope that would take them to the smashed outfit.

The wagon's stern had struck a huge boulder, partially up-rooting the rock but ultimately stopped by it. The boulder had lifted the rear end high into the air and set the bow down against the slope. This left a triangular space under the bed between the boulder and the bow. It was in this space that Fox lay, his left leg pinned under the smashed front gear forming the apex of the triangle, the rest of him free. The dead mule hung in its harness five feet below the front of the wagon, and its stench was already powerful enough to gag Craig as he and Irish made their way to the wreck.

"Fox," called Craig softly. "Fox?"

The man's eyes opened sluggishly, filmed and bloodshot. Craig had to call again, and, finally, Fox looked his way. Recognition formed in the eyes slowly.

"Craig!" Fox's voice hardly sounded human. "Craig!" A

note of hysteria raised its hoarse tone. "What'd you come for? You ain't goin' to kill me . . . ?"

His words stopped. The contorted expression of his face froze. Craig heard it then. The sinister, groaning sound. The small trickling of dislodged shale.

"You'd better lie still, Fox." Craig told him. "Looks like the slightest movement could dislodge the whole outfit."

"God. Don't you think I know it?" gasped the man. "How'd I get here? I swear that teamster drove his outfit off the edge to get me. It was so dark I didn't know which side I was coming in from. He jumped in time, but it caught me and my horse and everything. I must have slid down ahead of the wagon all the way till this rock stopped me. Then the outfit came crashin' in from behind and pinned me. Don't shoot me, Doc. There must be some way to get me out. Don't kill me."

Craig spoke quietly, trying to stem the delirious hysteria of the man's voice. "We've come to get you out, Evan. But I've got to amputate your leg."

Fox's head turned toward Craig. The man's eyes were so wide, Craig could see the pattern of blood vessels lacing the eyeballs. Fox licked his lips. Then he turned his head back to stare at the underside of the wagon bed.

"You mean it?"

"It's the only way."

The man licked his lips again and continued to stare upward in a fixed, glassy way, without speaking. Craig opened his bag and took out the instruments he would need, showing them carefully to Irish, one by one.

"You were right about someone to hand them in," he said. "If I had to grope around in my bag for them up under there, my hand would probably hit the wagon bed and set the whole thing off. This is a scalpel, Gabriel. I'll need that first of all.

You've seen those hemostats before. I'll use them to clamp the arteries. If we run out of them, this tenaculum might be necessary. Then this bone saw. If we have time, I'll use this catgut to replace the hemostats. Got that in mind?"

"Scalpel. Hemostats. Tenaculum. Bone saw. Catgut. How about bandages?"

"This sheeting I've cut into squares is for a compress," Craig told him. "Here's the carbolic acid now. Rinse each instrument in it just before you hand it to me. The same with the catgut." He looked into the other man's eyes. "Gabriel, if anything happens, promise me you'll swing out right away. No foolish heroics."

"It's a promise, Alan," grinned Irish, thrusting out his hand. It was damp with sweat when Craig took it. He turned back to his bag, getting out the collapsible tin cup, and wadded cotton into the bottom of this so tightly it would not fall out when the cup was upturned. He put this in his right coat pocket and in the other placed a flask of chloroform. They had lowered another rope down from directly above now with a small rock in it, providing enough weight to drop it under the wagon. Grasping its end, Craig started pulling himself slowly under that slanting bed of the freighter.

With his movement shale began its small, sibilant trickle once more. He saw Fox's body grow rigid with the sound. His leg touched a spoke of the smashed front wheel. He drew it back as if burned. The farther under he got, the more cramped it became, until he could not raise up at all without striking the wagon bed. Finally he reached Fox. He lay there a moment, panting from the effort, exerting a painful control to keep from coughing with the dust.

If he let go that rope from directly above, he would start sliding back again. He needed both hands to work, so he pulled the rope's loose end under his armpits, trying to copy Joliet's sheepshank. Then, hanging there, he fished the cup from his pocket.

"This is chloroform," he said. "It will put you to sleep. You won't feel any pain."

Evan's mouth worked faintly. "Doc . . . ?"

"Yes."

The man stared at the wagon bed above them for a long, silent space. "Nothing," he said at last.

The doctor saturated the cotton with chloroform and up-ended the cup over Fox's face. The man clutched Craig's shoulder spasmodically, lifting upward in a wild, startled struggle. His head struck the wagon. There was that sinister, squeaking groan, followed by that small trickling of rock.

Fox remained rigid, raised up off the earth, with his head an inch from the boards. The sounds ceased. Slowly, jerkily, he lowered himself back down. Craig pressed the cup against his face once more. He felt Fox settle into oblivion. "I'll take the scalpel now, Gabriel." He did not know how long afterwards he said that. "Two hemostats, Gabriel." Irish did not get the clamps to him quickly enough, and blood from the artery spurted up in his face, blinding him. "Tenaculum, Gabriel, I've lost that last hemostat."

Reaching back for it, his hand struck the wagon. Again that sinister creaking. He felt his arm go rigid.

"Alan," called Irish. "Those lines they've got hitched on it aren't going to hold. The weight's snapped one already. It looks like she's going."

"Get out then, Gabriel!"

"No. I've got my shoulder against the sideboard. She's still balanced enough so I can hold it. Crawl back down. We can both make it."

"You damn' fool," muttered Craig. He caught at that second rope above the knot he had tied, pulling himself up by it to give the sheepshank slack. When he dropped his weight against it, the knot held tight. He tried again. Once more the knot refused to come apart. He let go, pawing for his scalpel. With the blade poised above the rope, he realized the groaning had stopped.

"You still holding it?" he called to Irish.

"Yes, what's the matter?"

"I guess I didn't tie the knot right when I put that second rope around me. It won't come apart."

"Cut it with your scalpel."

"That's what I've got. Ease up a little first."

"Don't be a fool, Alan."

"Ease up, I said."

"All right, damn you. It's eased. I'm not braced to it."

"She's still solid."

"Like an eight ball on a pinpoint. One more touch and the whole outfit goes. Please come out, Alan. You've done your best."

"I'm half way through, Gabriel. You swing out. I won't need any more instruments."

"I'm not leaving till you do."

Knowing it would be futile to argue, Craig shifted back to Fox. He had to lie prone, yet keep his arms lifted off the ground to work.

At first it had been only the ache in his shoulders. Now his arms began to twitch. The spasm of cramp knotted up his hand. He straightened the arm out, dropping it to the talus with a heavy breath, trying to relax a moment. He felt something cool and hard pressed against his side. His fingers closed around a bottle Irish was handing to him.

"Usquebaugh," Irish told him.

"What?"

"Water of life. You seem to be slowing down a bit. If Samuel Johnson were here, I'm sure he would tell you that there are some sluggish men who are improved by drinking, as there are fruits that are not good till they're rotten."

The jaunty, unruffled wit of it swept the tension from Craig in an instant. He could not help but grin at the man as he relaxed flat against the shale, uncorking the Scotch, and lifting it to his grimy lips. The raw fire sent blood pounding through his head till he could not hear anything else. A new, heated energy filled him. He corked the bottle of whiskey, put it down nearby, and went back to work. He did not know how much longer it was before he finally got the leg off. He started binding on the first compress when Fox began to stir once more. Craig reached with his free hand for the cup of chloroform where he had braced it against a rock. His fumbling fingers upset the cup, and it rolled, tinkling, down the shale.

"Get it, Irish. He's liable to be violent if he comes out of it now."

"It's already gone. I couldn't catch it."

Fox stirred again, mumbling something. Craig went back to his bandaging, trying to finish up before the effect should wear off any more.

"Bowie!" shouted Fox suddenly, and raised up.

His head struck the wagon bed. A flailing hand caught at the gear. He shifted his weight against it, shouting incoherently. The outfit grumbled above Craig. Talus began its soft, dribbling sound.

"This is for good!" shouted Irish. "Get out of it!"

The dribble became a clatter. The grumble changed to the groaning creak of shifting wood and metal.

"Go on, Irish. I'll have to get my rope onto Fox. We'll swing out right behind you."

With the vertical rope still holding him in place, Craig caught at the harness Joliet had put on, holding it above the knot and shifting over to give it slack. As soon as tension left the sheep-

142

shank, it came apart. He tore the free rope from under his armpits, and pulled it under Fox's thrashing, struggling body. The shrieking, groaning noises were deafening now, and Craig could hardly hear Irish shout.

"Hurry up, for God's sake! That rock's coming out and the whole thing will go. I'm not doing any good now."

"I thought I told you to get out!" yelled Craig. Automatically, now, he found himself tying the surgeon's knot he had used on the ligatures.

"Alan, you damn' fool, you'll be crushed in there. . . ."

"Cast off, Irish. We're coming!"

With Fox fast, Craig rolled him over. Only that vertical rope held Craig now. He slashed at it with the scalpel in the same instant he pushed Fox out. Then he grabbed for the rope holding Fox and swung out with the man.

They slid along the talus for a moment with the freight wagon teetering high above them, its ironwork screaming like a woman in pain during that last instant of strain, before the lines holding it snapped. Then the rock pulled out with a tearing crash, and the whole thing went.

At the same time the weight of the two men had drawn the rope tightly enough to become a pendulum, and they swung out sharply from beneath the toppling outfit, with Irish pushing off behind them.

Craig's hands were scraped brutally against the shale as he rolled over in that arc. The noise of the wagon going on down the talus slope drowned out everything else. It flopped over and over, like a great fish out of water, until it smashed into timberline a hundred feet below. It lay there with the dust settling about it like smoke, and the landslide of shale and rocks still crashing down the drop after it.

Craig and Fox reached the other end of their arc and started to swing back. They were met in the middle of the backswing by Irish, coming down this way in his own arc. It stopped all three men, and they hung there against the shale in a huddled, gasping heap.

"I thought there weren't going to be any foolish heroics," panted Craig.

"Heroics, hell!" snorted the other man. "I just didn't want to lose a good bottle of Scotch."

Chapter Eleven

They reached Coffin Gap that Friday, riding back with the wagon train. A faster trip would have jolted Fox too much in his state of shock. He was taken to jail immediately and booked as an accomplice in the murder of Joliet's cousin. Asa gathered his carpenters and went to work on the hospital. It progressed quickly, for excavations had already started a week ago out on the heights east of town, and the foundation was laid and waiting for lumber by the time the wagon train arrived. Craig himself started back on his weary ritual, spurred on by the hope in that hospital rising on the hill. He was surprised at how many farmers and townsmen pitched in to help. The framework of the whole building was up, one wing walled in and finished completely, the day Coronet came to town.

It was Monday morning, and Craig was in his office, hoping for a free hour in which he could try and straighten out the mess his books had gotten into these last weeks. He had not been sitting at his desk long when something began to bother him. He focused his attention on the window. There was no sound coming through it. He had sat down to the usual clatter of early morning traffic, the creaking of wagons, the hoarse cry of a teamster, the clip-clop of horses. Now, there was nothing. He rose and walked to the window and saw it.

Bowie French had just turned in off Territory Road, riding a prancing, pirouetting copperbottom marbled with nervous lather. It was the best animal Craig had ever seen Bowie ride, and that fact alone was ominous. Behind him rode Ingo Hubbard, on that tall buckskin, and Mickey Daniels, Timothy Dunnymead, and half a dozen more of the Coronet riders. Now the

145

trot of their horses was audible. It lifted a sullen tattoo against the cottony silence, wrapping this end of Cutbank.

Gabriel Irish pushed through the batwings of his saloon and came to the curb, to stand in that expansive, genial way of his, thumbs in the armholes of his waistcoat, cigar pointed skyward, to watch them go by. For a moment Bowie's glanced crossed his. Irish smiled and nodded. Bowie did neither.

The barber stood in the doorway of his shop at Second and Cutbank, wiping his hands on a dirty towel. His motions had a hard, scrubbing nervousness. All the way down the rest of the street to the jail men were clustered on the sidewalk, or standing in the doorways. The silence of such a gathering was eerie. Up at Third a teamster had hauled his Murphy wagon in against the curb, twisting around up on his high seat to watch the oncoming horsemen closely.

Then Bowie was beneath Craig's window, turning his head up for one, deliberate instant to look at the doctor. It held the shock of a physical impact. There was no expression on Bowie's face. His eyes glittered in the shadow cast by his hatbrim. He turned his face forward again and was gone. Craig remained at the window a moment longer. Then he turned impulsively for his hat.

When he reached the sidewalk, Craig saw that Gabriel Irish was still standing before the Nebuchadnezzar and that another man had joined him. The doctor stared the other way down Cutbank, filled with the impulse to follow Bowie in that direction. But he saw Irish beckon insistently at him and finally crossed the street, and walked down toward the saloon.

"You don't have to worry about Bowie this morning, Alan," Irish told him. "That little show was just to impress us. He's not going to try to get Fox out by force. He's just come in to see his lawyers."

"How do you know?" asked Craig.

Irish pointed a thumb at the man with him. "You remember Chris Wren?"

Wren was a tall, gaunt, snoop-nosed man with the sharp, pouched eyes of an inquisitor. He had run law offices here in town when Craig's dad had died and had drawn up the bills of sale and contracts for the divestiture of the Scissors.

"I've been sent up from the Territorial capital to prosecute this case," he told Craig. "Fox is pretty jumpy. If I can convince him that even Bowie's power won't save him from this murder conviction, he's liable to let a few cats out of the proverbial bag."

Craig's attention sharpened. "How do you mean?"

"Bowie's gathered a lot of land up here during these last years," Wren replied. "A lot of cattle. Some of his deals have been pretty close to the shade. The stink of them has reached the capital more than once. There are a lot of interests down there afraid of his growing power, and they've been laying for him. If any of his deals have involved an actual crime, and Evan Fox were to give us the details, leniency might be given him on this murder charge for turning state's evidence. That's the angle I'm going to work on. Bowie thinks he'll gain by delaying the trial, but in reality he'll only fray Fox so much the man's liable to crack."

"I had no idea Bowie was that near the edge in his operations," Craig said.

Wren shrugged. "From the very beginning. Take your Scissors. That sale was to Laramie Grange, a company down in Laramie supposedly handling grain and beef. I've checked down there. None of the stockmen in the area has bought feed from them. The U. P. has never shipped any of their beef."

"What does that mean?" asked Craig.

"It's usually an indication of a dummy company, set up to

147

constitute a channel through which properties can be handled without revealing what truly happens to them. Do you remember the name of the president of that company? His signature was on your contracts."

"Beedle, Beatie . . . I didn't look too close."

"Emanuel Beebe," said Wren.

Craig frowned sharply. "Not the Emanuel Beebe who owns that livery out on Territory Road?"

"The same one," said Wren. "Who is also the brother-in-law of Larry Donovan."

"And Donovan is under Bowie's thumb," added Craig. "Is that the tie-up you're trying to make?"

"It's pretty obvious," said Wren. "Haven't you seen Bowie's beef on the old Scissors?"

Craig shrugged. "I thought he probably bought it from Laramie Grange."

"I doubt if he had to buy it."

"You mean he *was* Laramie Grange?"

"I doubt if he had enough money himself to buy Scissors outright, even working through Laramie Grange. Maybe Donovan helped out."

"But why should Bowie do it behind the barn that way?" asked Craig. "Why couldn't he come to me openly? I would have made a deal with him."

"Maybe he didn't want anything to start working in your mind," said Wren.

Craig's face took on the sullen, baffled anger of a young boy now. "What thing, Wren? What are you driving at?"

"Aside from the Cocked Hat, Scissors was the best spread in the basin at the time," the prosecutor said. "Bowie was the only one around here besides your father who knew you planned to go to medical school. It was a foregone conclusion that you'd sell the Scissors and leave for the East if something happened to your father. His death was pretty convenient for Bowie, Alan."

"Oh, no," said Craig heatedly. "Bowie isn't the same man he was when I left, I'll admit that. But I can't believe he'd be mixed up in anything like that, Wren."

"You didn't want to believe MacQueen was to blame for your father's death, either," said Irish.

"It's an ugly thought," said Wren. "Perhaps I shouldn't have put it in your mind. Or perhaps I should. Bowie's on his toes now, Alan. You'll want to be on yours, when he jumps."

He nodded good bye and turned down Cutbank toward the jail. Craig remained beside Irish, head turned down, filled with dark thoughts he was reluctant to explore. It took him a long time to become aware of the flush in Irish's face.

"You hot, Gabriel?"

The man shrugged. "Don't feel too good this morning, Alan. Didn't get much sleep last night."

"What happened?"

"Nothing. Just restless, I guess."

Craig took another look at his face. Irish tried to pull away when Craig reached for his wrist, but the doctor caught him.

"Let me take your pulse."

"Listen, Alan, I'm all right. I just. . . ."

"Take it easy, take it easy. Get excited, and you'll only make it beat faster. Just relax for a minute now." Craig timed it for thirty seconds with his pocket watch, then released the wrist. "You always have a fast heart?"

"Sure," grinned Irish. "Temperamental. Now what?"

"Just relax," Craig told him, putting one hand at Irish's back to form an opposing pressure as he pressed the other hand against the man's lower abdomen. Irish tried to hide the little ripple of muscle drawing up his face.

"Hurt much?"

149

"So would you, someone came along and poked you like that."

"Gabriel, I think you're going to be the first patient in that hospital."

"Oh, now, Alan."

"I mean it. You've got all the symptoms of typhoid."

"Alan . . . !"

"Don't make me take revenge for that time you socked me," smiled Craig. "Asa told me this morning that one wing of the hospital is ready to be occupied, beds, facilities, everything. The quicker we isolate you, the better. Let's go in and pack some of your things."

Over the man's irritable protests Craig herded him into the saloon. He sent Gentleman George for Irish's spring buggy and a saddle horse from the livery stable. When George returned, they were ready. Craig took the saddle animal, meaning to go on from the hospital to the patients he had to visit today.

The hospital stood outside town, on an eminence of the benchlands to the west. He found the north wing as complete as Asa had told him. In the room he made a more thorough examination of Irish and gave Gentleman George instructions for taking care of him.

"I wish I could stay here and nurse you myself," he said. "Actually, there's very little that can be done besides this rest, isolation, and a proper diet. I've left some antipyrin on the table. You can take it every two or three hours. I'll bring you some hot soup this evening."

"How about stimulants?" asked Irish roguishly.

"No good."

"Not even one little drink from the *caraba?*"

Craig sobered, meeting his eyes. Then he shrugged, with a wry, little smile. "I'll bring that this evening, too."

Craig noticed, in a pleased way, that the noise of the work

150

from the rest of the hospital did not reach this wing too loudly. He got his horse and headed down Cutbank, meaning to ride out Territory Road. Passing Ashfield's office, he saw that the Coronet horses were no longer there. He gave it little thought and put his animal into an easy jog-trot for the miles ahead. He was just beyond the turnoff to Coronet, within sight of the Fisher where it swung westward out of Kootenai Cañon and ran its turbulent way down into the Kootenai River, when a rider came up out of the river bottoms, pushing a hairy, little bronc' for all it was worth.

At sight of Craig the man drew his animal up so sharply it reared and wheeled under the pain of the bit. He hauled it down to poise there on the brink of the road, staring at Craig. Then he seemed to recognize the doctor and wheeled his way once more, galloping hard.

It was Timothy Dunnymead, the brim of his old horse-thief hat slapping hard in the wind. He came up so hard that he could not stop his animal till it had danced into Craig's horse. Again the reek of that kinnikinnick tobacco swept against Craig with all the other redolence of the man.

"You're the one I'm lookin' for, Doc," shouted Dunnymead, raucously. "This old gristle heel can't stop him. I tried, and he near cashed in my chips."

"Who?" Craig asked sharply. "What are you yammering about?"

"Bowie! He found out Nola had used her dad's insurance money to help you build the hospital. We was all in town when it happened. Lord knows how he found out. Bowie's like to tear Coffin Gap apart, hunting her. He found her in the general store. I thought he was goin' to horsewhip her right there."

"Nola!" shouted Craig. It made his horse jump beneath him, and he caught the reins up tight. "When was that? Where are they?"

151

" 'Bout half an hour ago. I been riding all over hell-and-gone, hunting you. They're probably just getting to Coronet now. I'm skeered what he's goin' to do, Doc. He beat her once. . . ."

Craig lost the rest of it as he wheeled his animal and cut right off down Territory Road at a headlong gallop, plunging into the silt-covered fields of the low ground there, in a diagonal line that would take him into the Coronet wagon road. Dunnymead did not catch up to him till they had reached this road.

"Where are the rest of them? Can't they stop him?" shouted Craig.

"Their guts has turned to fiddle strings. Bowie's swelled up like a poisoned pup. He ain't fit to eat on the same plate with a snake when he's like this. If I couldn't find you, I was going to try and get Gabe Irish to bring his gentlemen. I can't stand by and see Henri's little gal treated like this."

Craig booted at his animal harder. It was stumbling and wheezing with exhaustion by the time he came in sight of the Coronet. Bowie's copperbottom stood before the house, head hanging, beside Nola's stanhope. Her buggy team was still in harness, and none of the men gathered at one corner of the house was making a move to unhitch them from the stanhope. As Craig pushed his faltering horse through the open gate, two of the men detached themselves from the group and walked over toward the front steps. One of these was Mickey Daniels. The sun glowed red in his curly hair and cast strong shadows beneath the heavy bones of his jaw and cheeks. He took his solid stance by the tie rack, spreading the singular weight of his body evenly on his wide-spaced feet, allowing Ingo Hubbard to walk past him to the steps themselves, where he turned to face Craig, blocking the way. The doctor got off his trembling, blowing horse and walked deliberately toward the man. From the house came a muffled, crashing sound.

"What's going on in there?" he asked.

152

"I don't know," Ingo told him.

"I think you do."

Ingo leaned back onto his heels, tucking thumbs through his gun belt. "It's his house. A man can do what he likes in his own house."

"I'll go in, if you don't mind," Craig told him.

"I do mind."

In the murky antipathy filling the man's eyes, Craig saw that Ingo meant to make an issue of this, an issue that had been long in coming. He saw that he would have to meet it if he wanted to pass.

"I recall a day you spat in front of me," said Craig.

"And you told me you'd make me wipe it up some time," answered Ingo. "I always did wonder why you put it off."

"Get out of his way, Ingo, or *I'll* make you spit," said Dunnymead from behind Craig. "And it won't be tobacco juice."

Ingo and Craig must have taken the general attention off the old man, since, when Craig turned about, he saw that Dunnymead was the only one with a gun out. It was an old Joslyn-Tomes held across his saddle bow, pointed at Ingo and holding the other men with its threat.

"This'll mean your job, Tim," Ingo said.

"I reckon it will," said Dunnymead. "I reckon it's worth it to see somebody stand up to Bowie French."

Ingo's clothing rustled faintly against the reluctant motion of his body as he shifted out of the way. Craig went up the steps and past him without a second glance. Before he reached the door, there were more muffled, crashing sounds from within and Bowie's voice, raised in a hoarse shout.

"My own wife. Selling out to that damned second-rate pill pusher. My own wife! Come here, damn you. I'll teach you to. . . ."

153

The rest was lost in the crash of furniture. Craig caught the door handle, thrusting his weight against it. The door was locked. He rattled it violently.

"Bowie, come here and open this door."

"Get away, Tim. I told you, keep away," shouted Bowie.

"It isn't Dunnymead, Bowie, it's Alan Craig," yelled the doctor. A crashing sound from within, and Bowie's further shouts, drowned him out. He cast a look down the porch at the windows. They were all shuttered, but one of them was partly ajar, and he knew this could not be barred from within. He ran to it and tore the shutter open.

The room was littered with smashed, overturned furniture. Bowie stood down at the far end, before the fireplace, with Nola held in a sitting position at his feet. He had one hand in her long, black hair, holding her down on the grizzly pelt with her legs twisted beneath her. Nola's head was forced back against the stones forming the fireplace, and her eyes were staring up at Bowie, wide and black and depthless. One whole side of her face was still stinging red from a blow, and blood was trickling from a corner of her tight lips. She made no sound. It was the Indian in her. And with that blank implacability of her eyes, Craig found himself feeling almost frightened for Bowie, instead of for the woman. Apparently Bowie was too sunk in his rage even to hear Craig pull that shutter open, for he was yanking Nola's head back and forth, shouting at her.

"Say something, you damned squaw. I know you did it. The whole town's talking about you and him. What have I got for a wife?"

He drew his free hand back to hit her again, and it was then that Craig called to him.

"Let her go, Bowie."

Bowie released her and pulled his gun out as he spun around. Craig had not expected it to come like that. He felt the leap of

154

nerves through his arm in response, but it was too late. He could not even feel the butt of his gun against his fingers when Bowie's weapon came free. At the same instant Nola lunged forward from behind Bowie, catching his wrist in both hands and sinking a row of white, animal teeth into it.

Bowie's face contorted with his shout of pain. It incapacitated him enough so that Nola could twist the gun from his hand. He wheeled toward her, eyes squinted with rage and pain, to try tearing it out of her grip.

Forgetting his own gun, Craig jumped through the low window and dodged across the room to catch Bowie by the elbow and spin him away from Nola. It put Bowie off-balance, and Craig shoved him heavily against a wing chair. Bowie could not help going forward over its arm into the deep, leather seat. Craig came in on top of the man, putting a knee in his belly and grabbing his shoulders with both hands to hold him there.

"Let go, Alan," Bowie cried, twisting from side to side. "I'll kill you! I swear, I'll kill you!"

Craig's weight, and the way he had Bowie pinned into the chair, held the man. "Calm down," panted the doctor, shifting back and forth to block Bowie's attempts to free himself. "Calm down, Bowie. It's all over."

There was something primitive and frightening about the snarling gutturalizations that escaped Bowie as he continued to struggle. Craig fought him until the man saw that it was useless and stopped, panting heavily. His eyes, staring up at Craig, were filmed with silvery rage. There was no reason left in them.

"I knew you were capable of a lot of things," Craig told him. "I never thought beating a woman was one of them."

"Woman, hell! Tramp! That's what she is. Damned little half-breed Indian tramp! She can't ever be anything else. I knew that when I married her."

"Why did you marry her, then?" asked Craig. The soft,

questioning tone of his voice brought some focus to those silvery eyes. For a moment only the savage sound of Bowie's breathing filled the room, with the two of them staring at each other. "Was it an easy way to get the Cocked Hat?" asked Craig again in that same soft way.

It brought Bowie up in a surge, torso swelling with his wild effort. But Craig blocked it again. The two of them remained locked against each other, with Craig's weight gradually forcing Bowie down. Bowie sagged back against the chair.

"Never mind, Bowie," said Nola. She stood up against the fireplace, and the utter, unmoved calm of her voice formed a striking contrast to their violence. She was looking at Bowie with no vindication, no anger, only a vague, tired resignation in her eyes. "You don't have to hide it from me any longer. I guess I've known it a long time, really. Not at first. You made it all look plausible, then. I could see how putting the Cocked Hat beef under your brand would save a lot of work for the crews when it came to a drive. I even thought you were right in selling Dad's home and half of the old Cocked Hat pastures to Laramie Grange. It did look like they'd been ruined by silt."

"Did you know that Laramie Grange was a dummy company?" Craig asked her. "And that selling anything to them was as good as selling it to Bowie? So that put the land as well as the cattle in your name, is that it, Bowie?"

"Damn you."

"If you'd go that far, maybe you'd go a little farther. You were willing to kill a man in that attack on Asa's lumber. Maybe you've been willing to kill before."

Bowie's head snapped back, eyes staring up at Craig, wide and blank. Then he twisted over sharply, jackknifing a knee between them. Craig blocked it as he had done before, but this time Bowie threw himself backward instead of upward. It overturned the chair. Craig tried to follow Bowie down, bellying over the chair, but he had lost his grip.

Bowie rolled out from under, lashing out at Craig with his boots. It knocked Craig away. The doctor had gained only his hands and knees when Bowie came to his feet. Bowie charged with a wild shout. Craig saw the kick coming and tried to throw himself away. It caught him under one shoulder, knocking him up and over to go skidding across the floor till he came up against the wall.

"I'll kill you! I'll kill you!"

The screaming words rocked the room as Bowie came across it at Craig, that maddened blankness in his eyes. Craig's head was clear enough to wait until the last instant, rising part way as if to meet Bowie and then to throw himself aside. Bowie was coming so hard that he smashed face foremost into the wall before he could stop himself. The whole building shuddered with it. He reeled aside in a blind, pawing way. It gave Craig the moment he needed.

He was on his feet now, and he shifted back into Bowie, blocking aside one pawing hand to hit the man in the belly with all the weight of his body. A shooting pain went up his only lately healed arm, but he barely felt it in his anger. Bowie doubled over with a dull, hurt sound. He tried to grapple Craig.

The doctor gave him another vicious, hooking blow. It spun Bowie half way around into one of the chairs. He caught blindly at its back for support and then, in a quick, shifting move, swung it around between himself and Craig.

Bowie's eyes were still squinted with pain, and more pain was in the grunt of effort it cost him to lift up that chair. The doctor tried to stop it, but Bowie swung it upward viciously, knocking Craig's hands off. For a moment Craig lost contact with it, his hands stunned by the sharp blow of the wooden legs. This gave Bowie a chance to swing it back over his shoulder.

Bent down, with his upthrown arm his only protection, Craig saw the blow coming. He tried to turn his shoulder towards it, but the chair struck him full. It smashed his arm back into his face. Blinded by the pain, he felt himself going backward. There was another splintering blow across his head and face, knocking him into the wall.

He heard his own chesty, animal groans of effort as he tried to roll out from under it, but he saw that he could never make it. Bowie was once more swinging up that broken-legged chair. This time it pinned Craig back against the wall in a twisted, sitting position. The chair was smashed completely by the blow.

Craig had a blind sense of Bowie's bending above him after that, and of his hair being caught in the man's hand, to beat his head against the wall. The first impact stunned him. Then he couldn't breathe, and he realized his whole face was against Bowie's sweating belly. Making muffled, incoherent little sounds, he wound his arms about the man's legs and heaved forward.

He felt Bowie's long, driving legs lashing to kick free, but he hung on, pinning the knees, and Bowie toppled. He crawled over the man, yet unable to see, and started pounding for his face with a fist held like a hammer. His first blow struck the floor, and he cried out with the pain of that. Then he felt flesh and bone give beneath the second one.

Bowie caught his arm before it could come down a third time and used it to lever him over. They rolled across the floor, clawing, kicking, smashing into the furniture, until they reached the bear rug. Turning over and over, they got the rug twisted about them until they were both struggling in its folds.

Craig found his face buried in the filthy, golden pelt. Unable to breathe, he caught at it in a wild panic, trying to fling it from him and fend off Bowie, too. He saw the savage leer on Bowie's face, as the man released him. And then that was gone, blotted

158

out by the pelt once more, as Bowie caught it up and threw it across Craig's face again, coming down on top of it himself.

Craig was carried back against the floor, thrashing about beneath the pelt and the weight of the other man, wild with suffocation. Every gagging breath he took brought him nothing but a mouthful of fur. He tried to roll over on his hands and knees. Bowie caught him and spun him back, piling more of the pelt into his face. Things began to spin. Flashes of light burst before his eyes. There was a sensation of swelling that filled his body, till he thought it would burst, then a sense of constriction, so great he wanted to scream with it, and could make no sound. He felt his body thrashing in a last, wild attempt to free itself.

Then, somehow, his right hand worked itself through the folds of the pelt, and he felt Bowie's face beneath his clawing fingers. He found an eye and hooked a thumb into it.

Bowie's sound was muffled, almost ludicrous, through the bear rug. He tried to jerk away from Craig's hand, but Craig surged up, keeping his thumb hooked in that eye. Bowie could not maintain his weight across the pelt with the pain of it. Slowly, inexorably, as Bowie twisted away, their positions were reversed. The pelt slid from between them, fold by fold, until they were free of it. Groaning with the strain, Bowie finally got one elbow under Craig's forearm, levering it back. Craig felt his thumb slipping and released the hold suddenly, shifting his weight to strike at the man.

It rocked Bowie's head back. Bowie blocked the next one, getting to a knee. Craig was on both knees. They slugged at each like that, blows heavy and slow with their weariness. Craig came in against Bowie, hooking a hand under his knee and heaving upward.

Bowie went over backward. Craig tried to get to his feet, following the man, but could not. He fell back to his hands and knees, mouth slack and fluttering with the breath passing through it. Bowie rolled over slowly, painfully, and got to his knees. They crouched there, heads weaving back and forth feebly, staring at each other. Nola stood by the fireplace in that rigid, wide-eyed way, as if holding herself from interference, realizing they had to finish this in their own way.

With a rattling sound in his throat Bowie threw himself at Craig once more. The doctor caught him. They began striking again. But neither of them had the strength to make his blows tell. Bowie pawed feebly for Craig's face. The doctor could hardly lift his arms to block it. His own punch struck Bowie soddenly. He caught the man, trying to use him to get up, but as soon as Craig got to his feet, he fell against Bowie. The man went backward with him, and they were on the floor again. All Craig's strength seemed taken up with breathing. He found himself on hands and knees once more, staring through the soggy, black hair that had fallen across his eyes. His ribs ached so with each breath that he wanted to gasp with pain but did not have the strength.

"That it?" asked Bowie in a weak, husky voice.

"I guess it is," said Craig in guttural, weary frustration. "I can't get up."

"Looks like we can't kill each other with our bare hands," said Bowie. "Come back tomorrow, and we'll try it some other way."

Chapter Twelve

Twilight turned Cutbank Street to the texture of old tapestry. The traffic was still heavy at this hour, but its noise held a subdued, desultory pattern. There was the creak of dry axles from the tilting, grumbling Murphy wagons, hauling their inevitable way along the main street, the barber's tired good night as he stood in his doorway, watching a last patron leave, and the monotonous discord of a piano, echoing from one of the saloons.

It made little impression on Craig as he turned his horse in off Territory Road. He sat slumped in his saddle, sick at his stomach with reaction to the violence of the fight, stiff and aching all over. Dunnymead rode watchfully, nervously beside him, and from behind came the muffled rattle of Nola's stanhope. Between them they had gotten her out. Bowie had been too exhausted by the fight to make any effort at preventing it, and Dunnymead's gun on the crew precluded any action from them. Craig halted his jaded horse before the Blackhorn and waited for Nola to bring her buggy up to him.

"You'll probably be able to get a room here," he told her. "If Marcus is full, tell him to give you my room."

"I'm worried about you," she said.

"I don't think Bowie did any permanent damage," he told her. "If anyone's to be worried about, it's you."

"I'll be right outside her door, all night long," said Dunnymead, patting the butt of his ancient Joslyn-Tomes.

"I don't even think that will be necessary," said Nola calmly. "I think Bowie knows when he's lost something for good."

Craig gazed into her eyes a moment longer. Then his head made a weary, wobbling motion, and he mumbled something about seeing them in the morning. He knew he should see Irish before he quit tonight and wondered if he had the strength. Dully, almost aimlessly, he free-bitted the animal through the intersection of Second and Cutbank, trying to focus his mind on some direction. His beaten, numbed weariness made him almost silly. It was like an intoxication. It filled him with a fuzzy indifference to everything. When he saw a man beckoning him from the sidewalk, he failed to respond. Then the man was calling to him, and Craig kneed his animal over to the curb. It was Gentleman George, staring wonderingly up at him through the dusk.

"Your horse step on you, Doc?"

"Little trouble, George. Who's watching Gabriel?"

"Nobody. I just come down to get supper. Be going back in a few minutes."

"You left him alone?" Craig's voice held a lifting note.

"Well, what now, Doc? I had to eat, didn't I? The boss said it would be okay. Okay? In fact, he was the one who sent me down. He wanted me to pick up that ca . . . that ca. . . ."

"Caraba?"

"That's it. *Caraba*. He was afraid you might forget it. If you're goin' up now, maybe you can take it to him."

Craig took the straw-wrapped bottle George handed up to him. He looked at it a moment, filled with some obscure nostalgia by the knowledge of what had been in Irish's mind. He stuffed it absently into a saddlebag and lifted his reins. It was then that the explosion came.

The earth shook to the dull, booming sound, and Craig's horse snapped up its head and started to rear in excitement. Craig laid his reins against one side of its neck, bringing the beast back down into a dancing, pirouetting movement. It spun in a complete circle before he again had it in hand. Gentleman George was staring stupidly up the street toward the west end

162

of town. Smoke stained the twilight down there, gradually condensing into a definite, billowing formation that rose skyward like a mordant cumulus. A great, sick premonition held Craig idly in his saddle for a moment. Then he booted the excited animal into a headlong run up the street.

Men were coming onto the sidewalks all along the way and starting to run back and forth across Cutbank, shouting at each other and pointing at the smoke. At Seventh Craig had to rein the running horse hard aside to avoid riding down a man dodging out from the sidewalk. It was Ashfield, a napkin still tucked into his collar.

"Looks like the hospital's on fire," he shouted to Craig. "We'd better get up there."

Craig was already past, cutting around a rig that was turning in off the side street. He was only one of many riders filling Cutbank now. The earth shuddered to the pound of their horses' hoofs. The hot summer air muffled their shouts like cotton.

The street ceased to be Cutbank and became the wagon road that wound away into the benches. The houses and buildings of the town were behind, and the hospital came into full view ahead. Flames danced like laughing devils beneath the pall of smoke. The whole building was burning fast.

Craig was among the first riders to turn off the main wagon road onto the driveway leading up to the hospital. When the heat of the flames got so hot that he could not control the frightened, balky horse any further, Craig swung himself off the animal.

A silhouette appeared against the red flames, a bobbing, weaving silhouette, stumbling toward them. It was one of Asa's watchmen, holding a bloody head.

"Came at me from behind," he gasped, staggering into Craig. "I couldn't do anything. Lucky I didn't get blowed up in that dynamite. Them damned miners. I saw MacQueen himself."

"Where's Irish?" Craig shouted at him. "Did he get out of it? Did you get him out?"

"Who?"

"Irish, Gabriel Irish," Craig yelled hoarsely. "He was in the finished wing."

"I didn't know anybody was there, Doc," sobbed the man.

Craig let him go, wheeling to run on toward the hospital, trying to place the wing in the holocaust. A buckboard came rattling up the driveway, driven by Asa. He skidded it around to a halt, and Gentleman George jumped off, coming in behind Craig.

"You ain't goin' in there, Doc?" he shouted. "You'll never get out."

"Gabriel's still in there," Craig answered him. He cut off to his right, trying to find some hole in the fire through which he could gain the wing. The smoke was so thick he was coughing heavily now. He ran into Fields. The man was carrying a bucket, and it sloshed half the water out over the ground.

"Get a bucket, Doc," cried the stable keeper. "We're forming a line from the Hostetter well across the road."

Craig tore off his coat, wadded it deeply into the bucket, pulled it out, dripping. Then he wheeled back to run directly at the fire.

"Doc," shouted Harry Fields. "Don't be crazy . . . !"

"I'm comin too, Doc," Craig heard George call from somewhere behind him.

Craig veered aside from the smoldering embers of one of the outbuildings they had erected during construction. The heat was so intense he had to hold the wet coat over his head now. A wall fell in with a blazing crash, scattering flaming embers all over him. They sizzled against his coat and slid off in hissing

164

defeat. It was all a jumbled, undifferentiated sense of blazing timbers, crashing walls, and the black smoke, billowing up suddenly, unexpectedly, to blind him, to choke him.

He finally staggered against the finished siding of a wall, and knew this was the wing he wanted. Flames already licked up the unpainted boards at one end, but the row of windows above him was still untouched. As he sought a piece of board to smash one in, Gentleman George came groping through the flames and stumbled against him.

"That you, Doc?" he choked.

"Let go," Craig shouted at him. "We've got to break through those windows."

"I'll get 'em, Doc," the man grunted, turning blindly toward the flaming end of the wall.

"Not that way!" Craig yelled. "It's burning down there."

"Down where?" cried the man. He wheeled back toward Craig, squinting his eyes painfully and groping like a blind man with his hands. The wall began to groan and crackle above him.

"Watch it!" Craig yelled. "That wall's burning through. Get out from under it. Oh, damn you, George, get out of here and let me get Irish, will you? Just get out!"

The man turned directly in toward the wall, still pawing wildly. Realizing that the smoke must have blinded George, Craig ran at him. The wall gave with a crackling roar. George disappeared beneath the avalanche of charred board and blazing studding.

Craig could not help reeling back from it. His coat was burned through in a dozen places now, dried out by the heat. He flung it from him and ran forward again with one arm held before his face, seeking George. He saw the man heave up from under the fallen section of the wall, crying out with the pain of his burns.

165

"Doc, Doc, where are you? I can't see anything."

Craig waded into the smoldering embers, grabbing the man's shoulders to pull him away from the fallen wall. George stumbled a few feet, then went down to his hands and knees.

"Well, what now, Doc? I ain't much good, am I?"

"George, I'm going to point you out of it. You've got to go out yourself, understand? If I take the time to lead you, there won't be anything left of this wing. For God's sake, just go now. That way. The crowd's that way." He pointed the man in the right direction and then lifted his voice to a hoarse shout. "Asa, you out there? I'm sending George out. Come and get him, will you? He's blinded. Asa!"

On his hands and knees Gentleman George started crawling back toward the shouting crowd, soon invisible through the smoke. Craig turned back to a remaining wall, running down its length till he found a piece of two-by-four lying on the ground. With this he smashed out one of the windows and hoisted himself through.

The room he climbed into was not burning, but smoke had leaked under the door. Choking in it, unable to see, Craig stumbled across the floor. His pawing, swinging arms struck the iron bedstead. He veered away from that, finding the door at last. The hallway was filled with smoke, too. Through watering, squinted eyes, he could see flames licking through its blackness at one end. He knew the room they had left Gabriel in, but he had no sense of direction in the vortex of this maëlstrom. He went down the line of doors, flinging each one open, calling the man's name.

"Gabriel. Are you in here? Gabriel?"

"Here," came a weak reply. "Over here."

Following the sound, he found the man sprawled on the floor of the hallway.

"Alan!" Irish said feebly. "Whole room's burning. Had to

166

get out. Too weak to go far. Didn't realize typhoid made you so weak. Too weak."

Craig went to his knees beside the man, grasping him beneath the arms. The hot, crusty feeling of it surprised him, but he did not realize what it was till he got the man out. They crawled down the hall away from the flames to a rear window. Craig shoved it open and boosted Irish through. Then he climbed through himself, with the crash of more wall behind him. He hauled Irish away from the building, beating off the falling sparks, until he reached the edge of the crowd. Irish was rolling from side to side in pain, and Craig saw now how badly burned he was. He caught sight of Harry Fields among the circling men and shouted at him.

"Get some grease. Axle grease, butter, anything. Quick!"

Irish stopped that fretting, twisting motion, and opened his eyes, grinning feebly up at Craig. "I'd rather have a drink, Alan."

Craig's eyes were somber, staring down at him. "Asa," he said, catching sight of the man above them, "see if you can find my horse, will you? There's a bottle in the saddlebags."

"Sure, Doc," Asa told him.

Someone slipped a folded coat under Irish's head, and he relaxed a little, closing his eyes. "That's good," he said. "We never did get to toast from the *caraba*, did we?"

Asa came back, leading Craig's horse. The doctor went over to the horse, took the straw-covered wine bottle from the saddlebag, and returned. Squatting beside Irish, he opened it.

"You first," murmured Irish. ·

Craig tilted the bottle to his lips. Among all the faces watching him in blank question, only Asa's seemed to reflect some understanding of the ritual. After he had drunk, Craig lowered the bottle, handing it to Irish. The man did not reach out to take it.

"Gabriel?" said Craig softly.

There was no answer. Craig stared for a long time down at the closed eyes, the faintly smiling mouth. Then he turned up the bottle and held it that way till all the wine had run out of it onto the ground.

Chapter Thirteen

Autumn, it seemed, was born that year at the top of the Cabinets, spreading swiftly down through their shadowed cañons into the basin, staining the country as it came with its vivid hues. Up on the heights the ferns tinted the unending twilight a fading yellow beneath dense stands of fir. The fallen berries of the kinnikinnick made crimson stipplings along the wild mountain trails, and spruce cones lay like immense, swollen chestnuts on the lower slopes, crackling slyly underfoot. The yellow flowers of rabbit brush etched bright channels through the furry sage of the flats, and even the town seemed to alter its hues. The hoof-crushed powder of the dust filling Cutbank Street turned to a russet mantle, ruffling like fine silk in the wind that whined through Kootenai Cañon with its chilling presage of early snow.

Alan Craig shivered a little with that chill as he stood moodily at the window of his office, studying the sky for signs of that snow. From here he could see the charred, blackened remains of the hospital on the eminence west of town. The sight drew deep, bitter lines about his mouth, and he turned away from it to look down Cutbank in the other direction. Weeks had passed since the death of Gabriel Irish, but Craig still felt a deep, rankling pain whenever it came to his mind. He felt that he had lost the best friend he'd had here in Coffin Gap, the only one besides Nola who really understood him. The loneliness it left welled up in him whenever he passed the Nebuchadnezzar, or when he came home late, and there was no one standing expansively before the saloon, cigar tilted skyward, savoring the night.

Though Craig had fought the typhoid epidemic without the

hospital until there were only a few cases left, the enthusiasm of the town seemed to have been shaken by the burning of the hospital. He could feel it whenever he walked down the street, could see it in every patient he visited. They seemed to hold him personally responsible. Still at the window he shook his head defeatedly. Maybe he *was* responsible. He had pushed it so hard. Maybe. . . .

Some movement on Cutbank caught his attention, blocking out his thoughts. A wagon had turned in off Territory Road, driven so hard it slued in the turn. The lathered team came toward his office in a prancing, nervous restraint. The whole picture of it took him back to that first day he had seen Garnet MacQueen. *I'm crazy,* he told himself, *it can't be Garnet.*

The wagon drew up to the tie rack before his building, and the driver got out, muffled to the chin in a hoary buffalo coat, the broad brim of a flat-topped Mormon hat pulled down over the face. The high, biting wind ruffled the bottom of the coat against Levi's, whitened with age and use. Then, for an instant, the face was turned up toward the window.

Craig stepped back from the opening, a tight, breathless sensation constricting his chest. He turned around to face the door, unable to think why Garnet should come. He heard the muffled shudder of the rickety stairs outside, the clip of bootheels crossing the bare floor, the hesitation before the door. The panels shook beneath the knock.

"Come in," he said.

The door opened, and she remained there, gazing at him across the room. Even in this dim, wintry light he could see the stirring fluctuation of color in her great eyes, like sunlight picking up the underlying tones of a deep and restless sea. She took off her hat in a thoughtless gesture, shaking out the rich abundance of her auburn hair, blown into wildly untrammeled curls by the wind. Then she was staring at him again.

"Alan," she spoke at last. "There's no other way I can say it. I've tried to think of an approach all the way down the mountain, something I could say that would change all this between us, make it so I could ask you simply as a doctor. But there isn't any other way. Will you come back with me? Dad's awfully sick. I think he'll die without your help."

He was unable to grasp it completely for a moment. Then small, furrowing lines began to appear in his brow. He felt his chest constrict a little more with each breath. He found himself staring down at his hands.

"What are you thinking?" she asked.

"I'd have to touch him, wouldn't I?"

"Alan."

"I'm thinking that I couldn't trust myself," he said. He saw that his hands were trembling faintly, and he put them quickly to his sides, lifting his eyes to her. "That's what I'm thinking, Garnet."

She took a step toward him, eyes intense with the effort to read what was in his face. "It's incomprehensible to you that I could come after all that's happened, isn't it?"

"A lot of things that used to surprise me don't any more," he admitted.

She paused at the desk, putting down her hat. Her chin lifted. "Alan, when I first met you, you were full of a lot of fine talk about wanting to be a doctor, about wanting to take care of the sick, about not letting anybody or anything get in your way."

"Did I put it that way?"

"Now is your chance."

He turned his head to stare out the window. "You didn't know Gabriel Irish, did you?"

She came across the room to stand before him, speaking with a swift intensity. "Alan, you aren't blaming Dad for that, too?"

171

"Too?" he asked her incredulously. "Are you trying to say . . . ?" He stopped himself disgustedly. "I'm not going to dignify this with discussion, Garnet. Not when a dozen people saw Jada running from the scene. Not when a couple of his Giant detonators were found a hundred yards from the hospital."

The strange, blank disbelief in her face, as she looked up at him, shook something loose in his mind. She moved her head from side to side, saying: "No. No. He couldn't. He wouldn't."

"You didn't know?" That incredulity turned his voice to a whisper. She kept shaking her head from one side to the other. "Where was Jada that day?" he asked.

"Up with the crews," she murmured. "He told me he was up with the hydraulicking crews."

"Did he now?" he said thinly. He turned away from her and walked to the desk. He could hear her breathing, over there by the window. Then the rustle of the coat against her body as she turned.

"Alan . . . I had no idea, no idea. . . ."

"What's the difference?" he asked wearily.

"Jada didn't know Irish was there," she said in desperation, coming over to him once more. "Alan, if Jada did set fire to the hospital, he couldn't have known Irish was in there. He wouldn't have done it that way. How many people in town knew Irish was there? How could Jada know?"

"I suppose he didn't know I was on the road when he took a shot at me up in Kootenai Cañon, either," said Craig. "I suppose he didn't mean to kill me out there at the MacBell House. If he's capable of killing one man, he's capable of killing another. I've tried all the time to think that he didn't murder my father, Garnet. Now, I don't know. I just don't know."

"But not Irish, not a sick man in bed."

"Oh, stop it!"

The sharp, tired disgust in his voice drew her whole body

172

up towards him. The motion caused the edges of her coat to fall away from her breast. He was suddenly very conscious of its high, ripe swell against the plaid pattern of the shirt she wore.

"You've got to come up, that's all. I know he's a stubborn, ignorant, prejudiced old man, but he's my father, and he's dying, and you've got to save him. . . ."

"If this had happened before Irish was killed, maybe I would have come," Craig conceded. He looked down at his hands again. "But now . . . now. . . ." He turned partly away from her, chin drawn down in such a tension that deep, leathery furrows formed beneath his jaw.

"Alan," she said. The peculiar, small sound of her voice drew his head back around. He saw that her coat had dropped off onto the floor and, in a blank moment, found this strange. An odd, sensual look had entered her eyes, glazing one of them, for just an instant, giving it the appearance of staring off at some distance beyond him, while the other was focused on his face. It should have warned him.

"Alan," she said again, and her whole body arched up against him, with her arms slipping about his neck. For an instant the violent, animal attraction which had gripped him that time by the wagon rose up in him now. He found himself pinning her in against him with the hard, brutal circle of his enclosing arms. He felt her parted lips flare against his with the savage pressure of the kiss.

Then, like a small, sharp blow somewhere within his head, came the understanding of how the coat had fallen, and why. He pulled his right arm from around her waist, reaching up deliberately to put his hand against her face, thumb under the jaw, and force her head backward, away from him. At the same time he stepped back, against the desk. His voice may have sounded quiet enough to her, but his body was still trembling.

"You told me something once, Garnet," he said. "Not that way, either."

They both seemed to become aware of the other person in the room at the same time. It was Nola French, standing just within the door, watching them with wide, untouched eyes.

"If the door had been closed, I would have knocked," she said without apology in her voice.

A flush deeper than the color brought by the wind filled Garnet's face. "I'm sure you would, Missus French," she said acidly. She turned in a swift, sharp movement to pick up her coat. She halted the motion, as she straightened, to stare up at Craig. The plea started to darken her eyes again. Then she saw how bleak his face was, and it stopped. Coat under one arm, she walked out the door. Craig heard the stairs shudder to her descent and knew she must be close to running. He looked miserably at Nola.

"She wanted me to tend her father. He's sick up on the mountain."

"You aren't going?" Nola asked him. "There is a storm coming, Alan."

"It wasn't because of that," he said somberly.

She looked at him a long, sympathetic moment before she spoke. "Irish?"

He found himself looking at his hands again. "I guess I don't make a good doctor, do I?"

"Better than you think," she said quietly, coming over to him. "How can they be so stupid as to think you'd go up after all that's happened? That old fool would probably have a gun under his pillow to shoot you the minute you entered the room. You've tried too often already. The time comes when a man has to reach this kind of decision. Most other men would have reached it after the first time MacQueen tried to kill them."

He studied her a moment, a wry, sad smile touching his lips.

174

"You're a lot like Gabriel, Nola."

"He understood you very well, didn't he?" she asked.

Craig walked restlessly to the window, staring outside once more. "He had the knack of putting his finger on the kernel of a thing like this. He could always make me relax." He stopped talking to squint down Cutbank. At first he thought the powdery flurry was dust, raised by the wind. Then he realized what it really was. "First snow," he said.

She moved over to the window beside him, gazing at the somber clouds building up over Kootenai Cañon. "Early," she murmured. "Means it'll be a hard winter."

They stood silently, watching it come. The flurry was thickening, mantling the whole of Cutbank now, the whole of the town, sifting down into the narrow notches of the alleys, driven across the main street by the wind, to start building little conical drifts against the upright supports of tie racks, to begin banking up against the high, wooden curbs. A cowhand banged out through the batwings of a saloon, glanced quickly at the sky, and ducked for his horse at the rail. He unlashed his mackinaw from where it was rolled behind the cantle, struggled into it, and mounted quickly, to turn the animal down toward Territory Road. There was something lonesome about the little horse, bent into the force of the storm, mane and tail whipped by the wind.

The barber came furtively from his door, carrying a shutter to put up on his windows. He got it set and hammered it in with his hands. The rising wind muffled the sound. The whole picture had a muffled feeling, soft and unreal, like the warped, retarded movements of a dream.

Nola pointed to the mountain wagon drawn up before the Blackhorn. "You see. Even Garnet isn't going to try to make it back."

Craig watched the wagon a moment without speaking, and

then turned to pace across the room. He pulled his chair out and sat down, leafing through his papers idly. Nola drew down the window shade, cutting off somewhat the whine of the wind outside. In a moment, though, the sash began to rattle with the buffeting of the storm.

The swiftness with which these blizzards could come up in this high country always surprised Alan. He sat there listening to the subdued rattle in a dark, mordant mood. Finally he raised his head in a small start.

"I didn't mean to be rude, Nola."

"That's all right. A storm always makes me moody, too."

"How have you been? It's been quite a while."

"I've called several times, but you must have been out with a patient. I'm still in town, Alan. Got rooms at Missus Alvard's place."

"No trouble from Bowie?"

"Not the way you mean. He has most of the old Cocked Hat now. Why should he bother with me any longer?"

Alan shifted restively in the chair. "I should think he'd still have his pride. . . ."

"Not in the ordinary sense. He doesn't care what the people in this town think. Never did. I've got Christopher Wren working on a divorce. Bowie says he won't let me have it. I think it's out of pure spite."

"I'm sorry, Nola," he said. She did not answer him, and he looked up at her where she still stood by the window. "What will you do now, even if you do get a divorce?"

"How can I know?" she said. "What would you do?"

"I'd leave Coffin Gap for good," he said. "I'd go to some wonderful, bright, big city. You're young. You're beautiful. It will be easier to make a new start than you think."

"Will it?" she asked.

Her eyes were wide and searching, holding his. Something

about her disturbed him, and he turned away again, toying with the papers on his desk.

"Wren still pounding at Fox?"

"Yes," she said. "Bowie's managed to delay the trial again somehow. It doesn't bother Wren. He thinks it's only making Fox more jumpy."

"That so?" he asked absently.

"Alan, what's bothering you?"

He shrugged, rising from his chair to go over to the window and, raising the shade again, peered out into the street. There was a somber, lengthening look to the faint shadows beneath his sharp cheekbones, something savage stirring in his eyes. He saw that the mountain wagon no longer stood before the Blackhorn.

Perhaps Nola sensed the turbulent doubt in his mind, for she caught his arm. "You can't go, Alan. You'd never get through the storm. Use your head. You've done everything you possibly could for them, and look what you've gotten for it. You don't owe them this. Jada's done too much to you. He's tried to kill you twice, shot that beloved team of yours, burned your best friend to death. How can you even think of it?"

She broke off, staring up at him in a wild plea. Somehow his mind was no longer on what she was saying. He had turned to face her fully, realizing that he had never seen so much expression in her face before, realizing that at last he had touched her. The expression in her eyes changed. The fear, the plea faded. Her lips began to part. He had seen that happen before. There was a small, poignant expectancy in it. He knew fully what it meant now. Something seemed to be gathering in him. But it formed too slowly; it would not focus, would not become definable. After waiting a moment, her lips closed.

"If I had been Garnet, now," she said in a husky way, "you would have kissed me." He started to speak in protest, but she cut him off. "Never mind, Alan. It's too obvious."

"No it isn't, Nola. That's just the point." There was something tortured to his voice. He turned to walk away from her, running a hand through his hair. "I wish it were obvious. I wish it were clear-cut. I tried to think at first that it was because you were another man's wife. But I know it isn't that. I wouldn't be afraid to say what I felt for you, even under those circumstances. It's something more. I've always had the sense of something unresolved between us. When I left for medical school, it was that way. I came back to the same thing. It's hard to put my finger on. . . ."

"I don't think it was unresolved *between us*, Alan. I think it was unresolved inside yourself. If a person's in love, he knows it. What has lain between us is as simple as that. I think you've known where I've stood from the beginning. You've only been afraid to declare yourself, because it's what's inside you that is obscure. Why are you afraid to analyze it, Alan? To face it? Are you afraid of hurting me?"

"Nola. . . ."

"Then face it, Alan. I want you to. I've been waiting for you to do that. Make it clear right now, whatever it is."

He gazed at her for a long time, the fugitive emotions shuttling across his face like the shadows of wind-driven clouds over a countryside. At last, without speaking, Nola turned to the closet, opened the door, and took his mackinaw off its hanger.

"What is it?" he asked.

"You're miserable," she said. "You won't be able to live with yourself if you don't go up on that mountain. I can see it in you. I thought I should stop you, Alan. I was wrong. I want you to go."

He reached for her then. Dropping his coat, she came. It stretched back over the years, a fulfillment that stirred their souls and left them trembling.

Chapter Fourteen

Craig went first to the Blackhorn, but Marcus told him they had been filled up when Garnet came. Craig knew they weren't full, but he made no issue of it. If Marcus would turn her out in this storm, it was more than likely no one else in town would give her lodgings, either. He went from the hotel to Fields's Livery. The stableman told Craig that Garnet had not stopped there. That mean she was gone, and he asked Fields for a horse.

"Don't be crazy, Doc. You'll never make it up on the mountain. This is a blizzard. It's fixing to blow all the snow in Montana right down on the Cabinets."

"I can't help it, Harry. Give me that buckskin. It's got the bottom I'll need for this."

Craig kept looking for the mountain wagon on his way out but did not see it. His next thought was Brockhalter's. The storm had gained its full strength by the time he reached the store, and he was already numbed and weary from fighting it. Craig had to beat on the door an interminable time before Brockhalter appeared. He sullenly told the doctor that he had no knowledge of Garnet. If she had passed there, she had not stopped.

Beyond the store a pass broke through the uplifting Cabinets, forming a buffered, echoing funnel for the raging wind. It struck Craig full in the face, and most of the time he had to ride with closed eyes. Snow was freezing on his brows now, turning them to icy hedges. His nostrils were pinched and white, and his lips a thin, blue line, with all the blood whipped from them.

The road turned at the end of the pass to climb northward against the shoulder of a mountain. Craig could feel the animal fight for its footing beneath him, could feel when a hoof slipped on icy ground or sank deeply into the covering of snow. It was becoming increasingly hard to stay on the road. In many dips it was completely obliterated by the drifts.

The only sound was the storm, made up of the wind in its changing moods. Sometimes it came in thick, cushiony blows, like a gigantic flail beating the feather quilt of the snow. Sometimes it howled like a coyote. Sometimes it thrashed and roared like a vicious animal, raging in a trap. Craig's whole consciousness was taken up with the constant battle against its awesome savagery. He tried to keep his attention on following what he could see of the road. But he found his concentration wavering, narrowed into focusing on his struggle against the force of the wind that whipped the snow against him in solid phalanxes. Suddenly he pulled up, forcing his eyes open beneath frozen brows, squinting painfully against the wind as he stared around him. He had done this before — he would never know how many times — but had always found the road again. All he could see now was snow on every side. His vision was reduced to a perimeter of a few feet, walled in by that sense of powdery whiteness.

He shifted apprehensively in the saddle. Consciousness of movement came dimly to him, and he realized how numb he must be. He turned the horse around, trying to follow its tracks back the way they had come. The tracks were already blotted out. The animal responded sluggishly, reluctantly. He stopped it once more and sat there, finding a strange indifference within himself. He stared around blankly. Then he realized how dangerous this was and prodded the animal into motion again. He started circling. Still he could find no sign of the road. When his circle had become dangerously large, he tried to cut back across it to the spot they had started from. He ran into a stand of gnarled, wind-twisted scrub oak that he had never seen before.

Pushed in against them by the naked force of the blizzard, he halted the buckskin once more. It came to him with a small, sick shock that he had lost his way.

He sat there a measureless, howling space of time, struggling with the panic that stirred within him. He realized he could follow the one, good rule in a case like this — to go downward in the hopes of eventually finding a river course and following it out of the mountains. But that would be to give up. He knew an overpowering discouragement. He knew a deep desire to quit. It was at this moment that he saw his animal's head lift. It turned aside to whinny, a small, forlorn sound in the storm. But it was answered. Craig's own head jerked up as he heard the other whinny, like a muffled echo coming down out of the wind-driven snow.

He could not tell the direction. He wheeled his horse about, kicking at it. The animal shifted indecisively beneath him. He finally raked it with the spurs.

"Walk, damn you," he said hoarsely, and raked it again, pulling up on the reins at the same time. The confusing signals, and the pain, caused the animal to toss its head, whinnying once more. Again that answer came. This time Craig placed it and released his pull on the reins, driving the buckskin head-on into the blast of the wind. He passed the trees, climbing a steep, treacherous slope. He almost lost the animal when they plunged into a drift. For a moment there was cottony emptiness clutching at him and a sharp, panicky fear welling up in him.

Then the horse found footing again and started climbing. He realized at last that they must be going up the shoulder, with the road above them. He had an impulse to dismount and try to lead the horse. But the drifts were too deep.

He could see the edge of the road now and the dim, struggling movement. He could not define it, or hear any sound of it, but its shadow gripped him eerily, fighting on upward toward that unrecognizable goal. Finally they climbed over the shoulder, and he saw that it was Garnet's mountain wagon. She was at the head of the team, pulling on the nigh bit, trying to lead them in their struggle to haul the wagon out of a deep drift in which it had lodged. When she saw Craig, she stopped, staring in disbelief.

"Alan." Her voice came in a small, muffled way to him, warped by the berserk wind. He stepped off his buckskin and made his way to her. She stood staring at him another moment, then ran into his arms, sobbing against his chest.

He held her that way, a strange peace calming him. Finally she pulled back, speaking tearfully.

"I had no hope that you'd come. I tried to get lodging in Coffin Gap, but nobody would have me. I can't think of leaving Dad in this, anyway."

"What's the matter with the wagon?"

"It jammed into a gully somehow. The rains washed out the road here this spring. I could always get around the hole on the shoulder, but I missed my direction this time. The snow's piled in there pretty deep. How about hitching your horse to the wagon and helping?"

"If you couldn't do it with your team, there must be more than snow holding the outfit. Why waste the strength of our animals, Garnet? We can make it easier on horseback. The wagon will be doing this all along the way."

She nodded reluctant agreement. He unhitched the team, getting her lap robe from the wagon seat and folding it over to make a saddle for one of the wagon horses. He mounted this, and let her have the buckskin. Leading the other animal, they set out again.

Garnet knew the road better than Craig and pushed steadily ahead. They passed the first abandoned sluice, thrusting its whitened skeleton out of the storm from one side of the road.

Then they went under the flume MacQueen had used last spring, carried on those high trestles across the road.

These landmarks made but dim impressions on Craig. He was numb with cold and found an overpowering sleepiness threatening him. He was riding huddled numbly into his mackinaw, the weight of his body sodden and heavy against the struggling horse, when he became aware that Garnet had halted beside him. He pulled out of it with a great effort, staring ahead for the cause. Drifts, obliterating any sign of the road, were piled in great, snowy banks against the shoulder of the mountain. He saw Garnet's mouth moving, but no sound came to him. The puzzled, straining expression of his face must have told her he could not hear. It made him realize how much louder the blizzard had become now. She raised her voice to a scream, waving an arm heavily toward the drifts.

"Dangerous drop off there! Couple hundred feet of cliff!"

"We can't get in too close to the shoulder, or we'll get buried in those drifts!" he shouted back. "How about leading the horses?"

She nodded, getting stiffly off her animal, sinking almost to her knees in the snow here. He dismounted, too, floundering around to the head of the horse. He saw that its nostrils and eyes were caked with snow and tried to wipe it off with his gloved hands.

She led the way, bent forward against the force of the wind. He stumbled along behind her, hauling on the two reluctant animals he led. The snow fought him with incessant, urgent malice. In fear of going near the edge he got too close to the shoulder and slipped into a drift to his armpits. He saw Garnet turn and start to come back, but he waved her on.

He struggled out of the drift. The sudden release, when he finally freed himself, sent him to his knees. Crouched there, chest heaving with the exertion, he realized how tired he was.

183

It caused him a heavy, savage effort to rise again. Trying to save his strength, he leaned forward into the wind once more.

Garnet now was so far ahead of him, he could see her but dimly. His head lifted in vague puzzlement as her arm went up. He thought she was waving him back. Then he saw the turbulent motion of the woman and the horse. Her body was leaning, but not into the wind any more. He released his animals, floundering into a run, heedless of his own exhaustion and the drifts. He went into one up to his waist and fought out again, gasping for air like a beached fish. He could see now that the buckskin was struggling to maintain footing on the edge.

"Let him go!" he shouted at Garnet. "He'll pull you off! Let him go!"

But she did not let go of the reins, leaning backward against the weight of the struggling, slipping horse. She was trying to tell Craig something when he reached her, in a gasping, incoherent way.

"Caught around my hand, somehow. . . . Alan . . . ?"

He saw then that some swing of her arm, when the horse started going, must have whipped the reins into a half hitch about her wrist. The weight of the pulling horse was holding the reins taut and keeping the hitch from slipping loose. He grabbed at the knot wildly, trying to tear it free. But the stiff, frozen leather would not give in his clumsy hands. The buckskin was thrashing around wildly, jerking Garnet with every lunge. The animal was on the edge of the shoulder, its hind end down off the edge, rear hoofs clattering wildly at a strip of icy rock. Its front hoofs were still on the road. That and Garnet's tugging weight were the only things keeping the horse from sliding off completely.

Realizing he would have no time to take off his gloves, Craig grabbed the reins a few inches from Garnet's wrist, putting his own weight against them in a backward lunge to try to get some

184

slack. But the buckskin was too far off balance to give in this direction.

"He's going! Alan, he's going . . . !"

"Give some slack on those reins!" he shouted at her.

"I can't! He'll pull me off!"

Her voice was high with fear, and she fought wildly against Alan's efforts to haul her forward. His foot slipped on the icy rock, and he went to his knees, arms about her waist. The horse screamed in shrill panic, and its wild, sliding lunge, farther on over the side, almost jerked Garnet off her feet. It was only Craig's arm about her waist that kept her from going. He saw that there was only an instant left and slid his arms down to her knees, clipping them there. She swayed above him, with all balance gone, a shocked, hurt look to her face as she stared down at him and then toppled over.

There was that infinitesimal space of time when the reins slackened between Garnet's falling body and the slipping buckskin. And in that instant Craig gave his final, desperate tug at the reins, letting his body fall forward with Garnet's. He went flat onto the icy rocks, without knowing whether the slack had loosened the hitch enough to pull free. His chest and head were out over empty space, and he had a shocked glimpse of the buckskin going down, kicking and squealing, to disappear in the driven snow filling the cañon. It was only then that he knew Garnet still lay beside him on the edge, only then that the feel of her body penetrated through the thick mackinaw sleeve, and the numbness of his own arm.

Slowly, painfully, the two of them squirmed back from the edge until they were safe. He got to his knees, helping Garnet up. She did not try to move when she was on her feet. Her lips were parted, and he thought she meant to speak. But no sound came out.

"You aren't hurt?" he shouted.

She shook her head from side to side. She looked about her in a miserable, dogged way. Then she made a vague motion back toward where they had left the other animals. It seemed to take years of struggling back through the snow till they reached the spot where the horses had stood. And found that they were no longer there.

There was a great indifference in Craig as he stared at the empty, depthless snow. He could summon no emotion. It caused him a painful effort to summon thought.

"How far to your place?" he mumbled at last. She did not hear him, so he shouted at her.

"Couple of miles!" The wind swallowed her words.

"Same choice we had with the wagon!" he yelled. "Our chances of finding the horses are pretty slim! Dangerous to waste our strength!"

Without a word she turned in the direction of the mine and started forward. Craig would never remember the rest of that trip. He was conscious of very little, even as he went through it. He knew he was very tired — so tired it seemed he couldn't even hear the blizzard any more. Once in a while the berserk fury of the storm broke through his apathy, and he was conscious of being whipped and battered this way and that. Once, like rising from a deep, drugged sleep, he became aware of himself down on his knees in a snowbank, without any memory of falling, and Garnet was tugging at him. Next time it was Garnet who fell.

Then they were in the cañon, crossing the bridge, with ice already forming at the banks of the river beneath. From the bridge to the house was not over a quarter of a mile. He knew that. It was measured in lifetimes. It had no end. No beginning. Only the middle. Only the fuzzy, unreal sense of some ceaseless struggle against a malignant force he never saw. At last it was the bunkhouse, standing in the snow-laden fir, and beyond that the cabin, black and lonely against the cliff. It seemed to him he fell against the door and beat on it a long time with numb fists, before Washoe appeared, coughing softly with the chill, and brought them in.

There was a fire, and hot soup, and the cook peeling off their coats and gloves. The warmth revived Craig somewhat. He sat in a stupor before the fire, trying to thaw the lethargy from him. Then, from somewhere else in the house, came the song.

> **Oh, don't go up to Bullard's Bar,**
> **If you like to sleep at night.**
> **They wash their gold in whiskey there,**
> **And drink the dynamite.**

Craig blinked up at Washoe. "Jada?"

"Yes," said the cook. "He's delirious. Been that way since Garnet left. I can't handle him."

"I guess we might as well start on that," said Craig.

So it began. In a house shuddering and creaking with the incessant buffeting of the blizzard. In a darkened room with only the sullen, undying coal fire from one corner, burning in the brazier Washoe had gotten from one of the bunkhouses. Fighting the incredible deliriums of Jada MacQueen until Craig and Garnet and Washoe and Jada himself were all dripping with sweat and weak with exhaustion.

"Does he drink much, Garnet?"

"I suppose he gets his share, Alan."

"How much? Twice a week? Three times? Every night?"

"No, Alan, no. He's not a drunkard."

"I've got to know as close as you can tell me. He's got lobar pneumonia, Garnet, and he's got it bad. Alcoholics rarely survive it."

"He's not an alcoholic. He goes on a toot now and then. The last time he tied one on was about a week ago. That's when he must have caught this. I found him asleep next morning out in one of the adits."

They watched the fever rise, and drop, and rise again. Waited for a crisis that would never seem to come. And listened to the song. MacQueen seemed to know a thousand verses, and he never repeated one.

> **Oh, don't go up to Downieville**
> **They hung a woman there.**
> **She killed a man named Barnaby**
> **For cutting off her hair.**

And, if it wasn't the song, it was something from the miner's past, coming up to haunt him. Some of the scenes came through so vividly that Craig could almost see them. He didn't know how many times MacQueen took him back to that cave-in up at Virginia City. . . .

"That's the slide. That's the slide. Damn coyoters. So you wanted to be a coyoter? How can anything hurt so much? Feels like my whole face is smashed in. Somebody comin'? Jack, that you? Has to be. Nobody else would come. Don't come down, Jack. The fault ain't finished slipping. Going to shift again. No use in you getting caught, too. Damn him! Jack, will you go back? Damn you! Jack, I swear, if you come down, I'll lay a laggin across your skull. *Laggin, hell, I couldn't even move!* Jack, I'm all right. No need of you to come any farther. Be out in a minute. *Minute, hell, I'll be right here on Judgment Day.* How can anything hurt so much?"

MacQueen had his lucid moments, too. Then he would lie there beneath the tumbled covers, studying Craig sullenly from under his shaggy brows with an inscrutability foreign to him.

188

On the fifth night, however, he was sleeping quietly enough so that Craig and Garnet could have their evening meal together in the living room. Craig came from the bedroom to find her standing at the table, light from the oil lamp in its center, picking up the bright squares of her gingham dress. It lost its meager cheapness on her body. The nubile swell of hip, the proud depth of breast lent it indefinable richness. He halted to look at her, smiling tiredly.

"Do you realize this is the first moment we've actually been alone since this siege started?" he asked.

Washoe interrupted her answer, coming from the kitchen with a steaming platter. He hesitated at the door with a soft, restrained cough. Craig helped Garnet into her chair, then seated himself. Washoe served her plate first, and came around behind Craig to dish the stew out for him. Again Craig sensed that hesitation, and turned to look up at the man.

He saw the same expression he had surprised on Washoe's face down at Brockhalter's the first time they had met after Duncan's death, some fugitive fear that would not identify itself completely.

"What's the matter?" asked Craig.

"Nothing, nothing. . . ." Washoe broke off to cough. It had a hopeless, racking sound. Garnet finally rose and took the plate from the man. He put one hand on the table for support, bending deeply, thin body jerking with each spasm.

"I'll dish up supper," Garnet told him. "You go lie down if you want."

Still coughing, the man made his way toward the kitchen door. His eyes crossed Craig's as he passed. They fluttered and dropped like a guilty dog's, and he went into another spasm of coughing. When he had left, Craig turned to Garnet.

"What's the matter with him? He looks like he's afraid I'm going to beat him or something."

She put the plate down, shrugging wearily. "I don't know. He's changed since Duncan's death. Duncan meant so much to all of us, being the child of the family. It seemed to hit Washoe almost harder even than it did Dad." She gazed at him in deep concern. "Isn't there anything you can do for that cough?"

"Only the sedative I've been giving him."

"He's that far gone, Alan?"

"I don't know how he's lasted this long," said Craig, lowering his voice. "He let me examine him the other day. I wish you could hear those rales through my stethoscope. They sound like a railroad train."

"Bad?"

He shrugged. "One of the symptoms. Living around these mines, working the way he does, only aggravates it. He contracted it down in the drifts to begin with."

"I know," she said sadly. "I've seen too many of them with it."

"There's a man named Trudeau starting a sanitarium for this sort of thing at Saranac Lake in the Adirondacks. I wish I could send Washoe there."

"He wouldn't go. We've tried to send him away before."

Craig studied his food somberly, without appetite. "Perhaps it wouldn't do too much good anyway, at this stage."

This brought Garnet's eyes to his. "It's close?"

"Months, if he's lucky. More likely weeks."

She bit her lip and shoved her chair back, rising to walk to the window. Craig let her remain there a few minutes before he went over. She had recovered herself by then. With him standing beside her, she opened one of the shutters. Craig saw that the storm had ceased, and, though the slope was covered desolately with snow, a warm wind swept down the cañon from the north.

"Chinook," she said huskily. "It will have that snow melted by morning."

Another warmth permeated him, a heat from her body, and he turned slowly toward it. This brought him into contact with her hip, and he could feel the tremor running down her body. Without a word he took her in his arms. They did not kiss. She only buried her head against his chest, saying his name over and over in a small, incoherent way.

Then, simply and without surprise, he knew why there had always been that feeling of something unresolved between himself and Nola. Their friendship, the understanding Nola had of him, her insight into the very core of his nature — all this, and love itself. Perhaps a man could not see this until he actually felt love. It must have been in his face, as Garnet looked up at him.

"Alan," she said again, in a different tone, holding him now at a distance.

"Yes, Garnet," he said softly. "I guess we're through fighting each other . . . at least that."

Chapter Fifteen

After supper Garnet wanted a few minutes with Craig before he went back to watch MacQueen. However, she had been as drained by the siege as Craig and soon fell asleep on his shoulder. He carried her to the makeshift bed they had rigged in the living room, covered her, and then went back to MacQueen.

Glow from the brazier turned MacQueen's scarred face into a weird, bronze mask. His eyes stared at Craig in unwinking, burnished silence. The doctor lowered himself into the rawhide-seated chair by the bed, disturbed by the malignant study emanating from the old man. He wondered if MacQueen were lucid.

"Washoe feed you?" Craig asked.

"Not hungry."

"You'd better have something anyway. Little soup, maybe."

"I'll eat when I feel like it."

Craig tried to smile. "You don't sound so sick."

At this moment there was a small, scratching sound from the door leading into the kitchen, and Washoe pushed it open, bearing a tray. "Heard your voices," he said. "Been waiting for Jada to wake up."

He set the tray down on the bedside table. Craig stared at the man, bothered by a difference in him which he could not define. Washoe felt the attention and turned to face Craig squarely. His eyes did not falter. He held the doctor's gaze for a space, and then turned part way around, feeling for a chair. He seated himself carefully, staring blankly at the bed, with a pensive, gathering expression molding his emaciated face.

"That right, what you were telling Garnet, about me having only a few weeks, Doc?"

The rawhide seat creaked beneath Craig's abrupt movement. "Washoe, I. . . ."

"Never mind." The man's hand waved a vague dismissal. "I couldn't help hearing. It's something I've known myself for a long time. Any good miner knows when the vein is pinching out."

"It might not be that bad, Washoe."

"Don't try to make it easy on me, Doc. I got something to say. I been afraid to say it all this time, afraid Jada would kill me for it. Now I guess it doesn't matter if you do or not, Jada. Is that a sign of how close it is, Doc? When a man ain't afraid of something like that any more? When everything gets sort of calm and peaceful-like, and you just don't care what happens?"

"What are you trying to say, Washoe?"

Washoe took a shallow breath, gripping his knees tightly. "I fed Duncan, Doc, the second day after you operated on him."

It was a blow to the pit of Craig's stomach. It robbed him of breath. It brought about a kind of nausea.

MacQueen rose to his elbows in a violent, surging motion to stare at Washoe. The cook looked from one man to the other, the resignation gone from him now, his voice leaving him in a gasp, dry and husky with the imminence of his cough.

"Duncan was crying so. He wanted something to eat so bad, Jada. You'd gone out with the crew, and I just couldn't stand to hear him cry like that. So weak and feeble-like. I thought a little bite would give him some strength. I know you said not to feed him, Doc, but just a little bite. . . ."

"A little bite of what?" asked Craig.

"All we had was a bit left over from supper, some of that pasty Cousin Jack was always eating. . . ."

"His stomach was swelled up all right," said MacQueen. It was the first time he had spoken. His whole massive frame seemed shaken by the terrible, biting gutturalization of the words. Washoe stared at him in fearful fascination.

"I guess so. I guess I'm a murderer, ain't I?"

Craig took a heavy breath. "That might not have been it, Washoe."

"Don't be so good to him," said MacQueen in that awesome, rattling restraint. "You told us yourself it would kill Duncan to feed him."

"That's right," moaned Washoe. He seemed to shrivel, huddling back into the chair weakly. "I can't let you take the blame any longer, Doc. I had to get it off my chest. You can do what you like, Jada. I guess I'd be glad if you killed me. I guess I'd deserve it."

MacQueen remained raised up on his elbows that way, staring at the man. Craig watched Washoe with a new understanding of the strange, furtive guilt he had been seeing in the man's eyes whenever they met. Then MacQueen made some small shift beneath the covers. Craig twisted toward him sharply.

"Never mind," said MacQueen, lowering himself down heavily. "I ain't goin' to do anything." He lay there, staring ahead of him at nothing, for a long time.

Soundless tears were running down Washoe's cheeks now. Craig did not know whether it was relief or sheer weakness. The man seemed to have aged ten years in the last moments. His eyes were sunken, his cheeks pulled in, till his head looked like a skull.

Finally MacQueen drew a whistling breath through his teeth. "I guess I got a little piece to speak, too. I've had a chance to think a lot, lying here, when my head was clear. This sort of caps it off. I've been wrong, haven't I, Doc? All the way down the line, I've been wrong."

The unexpectedness of it left no speech to Craig. He stared at the man, unable to answer in that moment.

MacQueen tossed his head in a fretting way. "You don't have to answer. I know. I couldn't believe you hadn't come back for revenge. Garnet told me what you said to her at Brockhalter's. That you hadn't heard the talk about me killing your father till you got back here, and that even then you didn't want to believe it. How do you feel now, Doc?"

Craig shook his head from side to side. "I don't know, Jada. I don't know."

"I do," said MacQueen. "I think that way down inside you believe I killed your dad. And thinking that, you still come up here. Through the worst blizzard this country's seen in years. Knowing you were just as liable to die in it as not. And all that, after I'd tried to kill you twice. I never beat a man as bad as I beat you down at the MacBell House, Doc. And those horses. I know how you felt about them. I saw your face that day in Kootenai Cañon. And . . . and. . . ."

There seemed a reluctance in him to finish. Knowing what was in his mind, Craig supplied it softly.

"Irish?"

"Yeah." MacQueen stirred restlessly under the covers. The heat left his voice, and it held a weary huskiness. "That's it."

Craig realized that his hands were locked together, and he separated them carefully, asking: "Just tell me one thing, Jada. Did you know Irish was in the hospital when you blew it up?"

There was a small pause before MacQueen answered.

"No, Doc."

The silence, after that, held them all. Finally, MacQueen shifted in the bed again.

"So that's it," he said. "I've always been a stubborn man, Doc. I worked with my hands more than my head. Whatever I learned had to be beat into my mind. I guess it made me worse to lose Duncan that way. It twisted my thinking. He and Garnet were the only things I had outside my mines. I couldn't think straight. All I knew was that you had cut him up, and he died. There had been talk for years that I'd killed your dad, and I thought you were getting back at me. I guess nothing else in the world could have convinced me how wrong I was except what you did here. Coming up through the storm like that . . . still thinking I had killed your dad . . . coming up after all I'd done to you . . . to save my life."

"I never intended . . . I never hoped to hear this from you, Jada."

"I guess not. It's the first time I ever apologized to a man in my life. And it isn't an apology, really. I know nothing I can say will ever wipe out what I did to you. I just wanted you to know. I realize how wrong I've been, Doc, and I wanted you to know."

There was something infinitely weary about the way his head sank into the pillow.

Smiling, Craig rose to his feet. "You feel like a little nap?"

"Yeah. I'm tired now. I'm very tired."

MacQueen's eyes were already closed. Craig nodded at Washoe. The two of them moved out into the living room. Washoe's face twisted up, and he started to say something. Craig put a hand on his shoulder.

"Never mind, Washoe. It's all over now."

The man sniffled and turned to go into the kitchen, coughing weakly. Craig took a seat before the coals of the fire. Garnet was still asleep on the bed across the room. He must have dozed himself. He came to with a start to hear MacQueen mumbling something from the other room. He went hurriedly in there to find the man hot and feverish again, talking deliriously to himself. Craig gave him a sedative, but it failed to soothe him. He had the sinking premonition of another violent session. MacQueen thrashed around wildly, calling to Cousin Jack. Then he broke into that song.

Craig worked with him till dawn crept into the room, sick

and gray. He was still there when a knock shook the front door. MacQueen had quieted somewhat, and Craig took the chance of leaving him for a moment. Garnet was stirring sleepily on the bed as he passed through the living room. He opened the door to find Nola French standing there.

Craig stared at her, not trying to hide his surprise. In that instant she spoke. He was dimly aware of her stanhope drawn up at the steps of the porch and of laboring breath swelling the gleaming, sweaty barrels of the buggy team.

"Alan," her voice escaped her thinly, holding a tremor of restraint, as if she were blocking a natural impulse to cry out, "Chinook's turned everything to water. I could hardly make it through. The road's washed out in so many places."

"What is it?" he asked with an intense wish to help her say it.

"The Kootenai's flooded, Alan. Most of Coffin Gap is three feet under water already. The only reason I could get out is that the Alvard place is on high ground. Coronet's covered, too. Dunnymead came out to Alvards' to tell me this morning, about four. Bowie's in one of his rages. He's coming up on the mountain, and he's going to finish it once and for all."

"Finish it?" Craig felt his whole body contract as the full implications of that struck him. "But he can't. MacQueen's a sick man, in bed. . . ."

"Sick, hell!" said Jada MacQueen from the door of the bedroom.

Craig wheeled to see him standing there, a swaying, hollow-eyed apparition in his nightshirt and pants.

"I can handle the lot of 'em. Tell 'em I'll be down in the mine. That's where they'll have to come if they want me. Down in the Jada Hole. Come on, Cousin Jack."

"Jada," cried Craig, "you can't do that. You're delirious. Go out there and it *will finish* you. You can't. . . ."

"No man tells me what I can or can't do!" roared Mac-Queen, wheeling drunkenly about. "I'll flood 'em out! Tell 'em to come down on me if they dare! I'll drown 'em like rats! Come on, Jack!"

The shouting had wakened Garnet completely. She threw the covers from her, sleep shocked from her face. Jada's uncertain, tramping passage through the bedroom shook the whole house. Craig stopped to grab his gun from the belt where it hung, jamming it in the waist of his trousers, and then ran into the bedroom to stop the man. MacQueen had already flung open the door, leading to the kitchen, and was in there.

"Stop him, Washoe!" shouted Craig. "Don't let him get outside!"

There was a shuddering crash, that sound of tramping passage on through the puncheon of the kitchen, the slapping slam of the back door. Craig reached the kitchen to find Washoe huddled down against the wall where MacQueen had thrown him. The doctor ran on out with Garnet coming behind him.

"How can he flood the place?" Craig panted at her, as they scrambled up the slope after MacQueen. "You don't have pumps in there, do you?"

"Dad's known Bowie would be up sooner or later," she told him. "He fixed it up that way a long time ago so he could flood the mines if they came after him. He's got piping in there and a monitor all set up. He's crazy, Alan. He'll pull the whole thing down on them. He'll drown himself along with everybody else!"

She broke off to stare behind her. Craig saw them too, coming up out of the timber no longer covered by snow. Apparently the three of them had pushed ahead of the Coronet riders. Bowie French was on his copperbottom, and the thin, wheezing pain of its labored breathing telling how hard he had forced the animal. Ingo Hubbard and Mickey Daniels trailed him, and they were the only ones Craig could see. He realized he could never get MacQueen if the man flooded the adits, and it made him put forth a last, bursting effort to get up that slope. He outdistanced Garnet, reaching the adit ahead of her.

MacQueen made a thudding, rattling sound within the passage. Craig called to the man, but there was no answer.

His eyes did not accustom themselves to the darkness at once, and he fell on his face within the first few feet. Before he started going again, he listened for MacQueen. There was no sound from ahead, and Craig remembered that winze he and Garnet had used before to climb from a lower level to this one. If MacQueen was using that, his sounds would be muffled. He was surprised that he could see a little now. It struck him why.

When they had used this tunnel before, it had been early afternoon, with the sun already dropping behind the mountain above. It was morning now, with the sun's light coming from the east and carried directly into the mouth of the tunnel. He no longer had to move blindly and reached the winze in a few minutes. Crouched there, the shock of Bowie's voice stiffened his whole body.

"MacQueen," called the man from the mouth of the tunnel. "Come out, or we'll come in and get you."

"Bowie!" Craig called to him. "Don't do this. MacQueen's a sick man. He's in no shape to defend himself. Let me talk with you, Bowie."

"I'm through talking, Alan. I've been trying to do that with MacQueen too long. This flood's ruined my land. What it hasn't washed away, it's covered with silt from your old Scissors up to my very doorstep. It's all MacQueen's doing. We're running him out of the country."

"You know he won't let you do that. You'll have to kill the man to put your hands on him."

"That's up to him. I shouldn't do it, Alan, but I'll give you this last chance to step off. Walk out here with your hands up, and I'll let you go alive."

Craig could hear the guttural, bestial tone of Bowie's voice and knew how close to explosion the man was. For that moment all he could hear was his own breathing, filling the drift with the abrasive rust of its sound. Then he called to Bowie.

"I'm not going to let you do this to a sick man. I'm not coming out."

"Then I'm coming in."

It was almost a scream from Bowie. Craig had never heard so much rage racking a human voice. Everything else seemed to break loose with it. The shrill whinny of horses, the shouting of the men outside, and then the first shot. It was lost immediately in the multiplication of its own echoes that rolled against Craig in a deafening tide, pierced by the scream of the bullet's ricochet as it struck a rocky wall. Other shots joined it, a whole volley of them, until Craig's consciousness seemed filled with one incessant explosion.

He pulled his own gun and started seeking the protection of the winze. His foot found the first step of the ladder, and he lowered himself on down, squinting his eyes at the terrible racket. There was the scream of another ricochet and a stunning pain in his right hand.

He felt his gun fly from numb fingers and almost fell himself. He pawed wildly with his left hand for a rung of the ladder, and then dropped on down beneath the level of the tunnel floor. His gun must have fallen to the next floor level beneath him, and he climbed down as swiftly as possible, going to his knees and pawing about for it in the dim light. Feeling was returning to his right hand, and he could not sense a bullet wound. He realized a ricochet must have struck his gun, knocking it from his fingers.

The shots had ceased from above now. How soon would they be coming in then? His hunt for the gun took on a desperation. And he could not find it.

He stopped trying at last, raising his head to look down this drift. The light grew feeble back there, barely reaching a turn in the tunnel. He knew there would be no light beyond that. It was the only way MacQueen would go.

Craig rose to his feet, reeking of the dank earth that dripped from his hands, his trousers. He followed backward the line of rusting rails. Paralleling the rails was a three-inch pipe, leading him around a turn. Sight was cut off abruptly. He halted, trying to hear something ahead. A rattle? A faint rattle?

"Jada," he called softly.

"That you, Bowie?" MacQueen's booming voice startled Craig. "Come on. I'm waiting. I'm waiting!"

He's reached the monitor then, thought Craig. *Enough head to blow the mountain down? What will it do to a man? Only one chance. If he's delirious. . . .*

"Jada, it's me, Alan Craig."

"Craig? You've come back to kill me. I know what they're saying in town. You won't touch Duncan, not *my* son, not a Craig. Come around that corner and I'll blow your head off. You won't touch my son. Come on, come on!"

He was delirious, then, and time was mixed up for him. Craig could almost see that crazed, red-headed giant, reeling over the ugly snout of the monitor, setting like a three-legged spider in the black earth of the tunnel. The doctor drew a deep breath and began to walk forward, singing in a loud voice:

> **Oh, don't go up to Bullard's Bar**
> **If you like to sleep at night.**
> **They wash their gold in whiskey there. . . .**

"Jack?" MacQueen's voice had a puzzled sound. "Jack, is that you?"

Craig tried to imitate Cousin Jack's rusty voice. "Sure is, Jada. Come to help you finish the pasty."

"Not a minute too soon. Come back here, Jack. French is out there with Coronet. I've got so much head on this thing, he'll think he was caught in a Chili mill. . . ."

Craig walked on into the blackness, humming softly at the song under his breath. He heard the faint clank of metal from ahead, the sucking shift of boots in muddy earth.

"Easy, Jada," he said. "Jack's comin'. Easy. . . ."

"Jack?"

"Yeah, yeah."

Craig stumbled against the metal legs of the tripod, almost falling. He was caught by MacQueen's immense hands. The man ran callused fingers across his face. They stopped at his eyes. Craig knew how much Jack's eyes would have protruded, even closed.

"You ain't Jack!" roared Jada.

He released Craig. The doctor sensed him grabbing for the stopcock on the monitor. He threw himself at MacQueen, going into the massive body, carrying it backward. The smell of the man — the nauseating reek of tobacco and heated sweat that never seemed to leave MacQueen — took Craig back to that moment when they had been locked together before at the MacBell House. His lunge threw MacQueen back against the wall of the drift, and for a moment the man's ferocious might lifted against Craig as savagely, as destructively, as it had that other night so long ago.

Craig hung on, knowing it could not last long. MacQueen tried to roll him over. Craig blocked that with a leg. MacQueen's grimy, ridged fingers sought his throat. Craig got a bent arm up to force the hand back. MacQueen was arched up beneath him for one last instant. Then he collapsed, all the sand draining out of him with the weakness of his long illness, and lay like an emptied sack of grain beneath Craig, breathing feebly, shallowly.

"Jack," he moaned. "French is out there. Get him, Jack. I'm done in."

Craig crawled off him, seeking the monitor in the darkness. Finding it, he crouched weakly over the tripod, drained of life in that moment by the intense struggle. When his strength began to return, he felt about for the stopcock. There was a length of crinoline hose between the metal piping and the nozzle. Amid the iron rings, strengthening the hose, he could feel the heavy canvas, swollen and damp with the pressure of the water. The nozzle was aimed at the tunnel where it turned, and all he could do was wait. Finally the voices began to come.

"I know I hit him, Bowie." *Ingo Hubbard?* "I heard him yell."

"There's some kind of hole here." *That was Mickey Daniels.* "It must go down to the next level."

Bowie did not answer. There was a furtive, sliding movement. The trickling clatter of dislodged earth. Then the scraping of boots against those iron rails.

"Here's somebody's gun," said Ingo. "I kicked it out from under that pipe."

There was a moment of silence, and then Bowie's voice came at last, filled with a guttural, flat finality. "That's Alan's Remington."

The utter lack of sound that followed was eloquent enough. Craig knew what was in their minds now. He was back here somewhere, unarmed.

The first sound of their steps reached him. They came on steadily, unremittingly. He could feel his ribs swelling with accelerated breath. He found himself licking his lips and stopped it. Then the first silhouette came into the faint illumination at the turn.

Craig's hand tightened on the stopcock. It cost him a definite effort to keep from turning it. The tension of the waiting seemed to swell within him till he thought he would burst with it.

Another silhouette appeared.

He could not recognize them. They came into view, shadowy outlines staining the vague illumination for a moment, then disappearing into the darkness on this side of the turn. He wondered if they could hear his breathing. He wondered if they could hear his heart.

The third silhouette appeared.

Craig's hands made a spasmodic movement against the cock, twisting hard. Washers creaked in the valve. There was a coughing sound, and the water shot from the nozzle. He heard it splatter against the wall. The sound was not loud enough to mean much force, and he grabbed the cock in both hands, twisting desperately. The pipe was clanking all the way down the tunnel now, and Bowie's voice rang out.

"He must have one of those monitors down here. Get back before it blows us all out."

The rusty valve twisted grudgingly in Craig's sweaty grip. He saw one figure tumble around the corner. A second. Then the cock slipped around completely, and the water began tearing earth out of the walls with a deafening, splattering sound. He grabbed the nozzle, pulling it around till the stream of water was pointed right at the turn, catching the third figure as it came into silhouetted view, running backward.

"Bowie!" screamed Ingo Hubbard. The rest of it was blotted out by that wild flood of water, carrying him back against the wall and pinning him there.

Craig knew that he would bring the tunnel down about them if he let it go too long, and he began twisting the stopcock back. As the stream of water died, a shot rocked the drift. There was the clang of metal on metal, the scream of ricochet. Before the second one came, Craig knew what they were doing. If they

204

could put a hole in the pipe, it would rob him of pressure. He knew that eventually they could do that, then come back, and get him without any trouble.

His eyes sought Ingo Hubbard out there. He made out the man lying in a sodden, broken heap against the wall, in the faint illumination of the turn. On a low ledge across the tunnel, metal gleamed dully. *His gun?*

Craig glanced in MacQueen's direction. He could not see him. The man was making feeble, moaning sounds. Craig called to him softly. There was no answer. More shots filled the drifts with their clapping thunder. Realizing he had only a moment longer, Craig crawled around the monitor and moved up the drift toward Ingo. He ran when the shots drowned his noise. He stood panting and sweating in the lull. He reached the turn during a volley, eyes pinned on Ingo's gun. He would be visible when he stepped out there. He would have just that instant, while they were intent on that pipe.

The shots stopped for a moment. *They must be reloading.* His indrawn breath seemed to scrape across his throat. Then his head jerked to the clamor again of gunfire. Bent forward, Craig ran out past Ingo Hubbard and scooped at the gun which had been knocked from the man's hand when the flood smashed into him. Craig prayed that the shells would be dry. They hadn't been — that time at the bridge.

Mickey Daniels stood behind Bowie. He was turning toward Craig, but his gun was still pointed at the pipe. Bowie had already seen Craig. His lips pulled back against his teeth, as he whipped his gun around, till he almost seemed to be smiling in that last moment when Craig desperately pulled the trigger.

There was one shot. Bowie remained standing until its echoes died, with that strange, wolfish leer fixed on his face. Then he pitched forward across the rusty tracks.

"Daniels?" said Craig.

The Irishman looked at Bowie's body for a long time without moving, without lifting his six-shooter from where it was still pointed at the pipe. Then he said: "I'm through, Craig."

"Drop your gun," the doctor told him.

There was something final to the thud of it, hitting the earth.

A scrambling noise from the mouth of the adit came to Craig. Garnet called his name.

"It's over," he told her tiredly. "You can come in."

She came in a stumbling run past Daniels to stop before Craig, clutching at his elbows and staring up into his face.

"You're all right? They didn't hit you?"

"I'm all right. You'd better see to your father."

Nola French came in more slowly, a tall, somber figure in her wine-colored suit. She stopped where Bowie had fallen, to look down on him for a moment. There was no expression on her pale face. Finally her eyes lifted, pausing at Ingo Hubbard's broken body.

"Dead?" she asked.

"I never thought those hoses packed such a pressure," Craig said.

"Do you believe in poetic justice?" she asked.

"How do you mean?"

"Ingo Hubbard was the man who killed your father."

He did not speak for a long time. His eyes sought Ingo's body in a fugitive glance. He was surprised at the lack of emotion in him. *Poetic justice?*

"Evan Fox confessed yesterday," Nola continued. "I didn't have a chance to tell you before. Chris Wren convinced him that Coronet was not strong enough to get him off, and that, if anything Fox could tell would implicate Bowie in an actual crime, Fox might get leniency for turning state's evidence. One of the things he told was of the deal between Ingo and Bowie. Ingo had been the partner of Christians. Bowie knew he was

206

out to revenge your killing of Christians. No money was actually passed between them, but Bowie let Ingo know that he would shield him if it happened to be your father Ingo reached first. Ingo knew Bowie's plans for getting big and saw Scissors as a foothold. Ingo could use the protection of a man who stood eventually to gain as much power in this country as Bowie planned to. So your father was shot out on the range, and you sold out and went East, and Ingo Hubbard was the first man to sign on at Coronet."

"Pretty vague evidence for a court of law," he said.

"I guess it doesn't matter now, does it?" she murmured.

"Alan," called Garnet from farther back in the drift. "Dad's head is clear now. Can I have some help with him?"

"Will you do the honors, Daniels?" said Craig. "I'd like to keep my eye on you."

Sullenly Daniels passed them, helping Garnet raise the miner up off the floor and walk him out. When MacQueen saw Bowie, he halted, sagging against a wall to stare down at the man. Finally he looked up at Nola.

"You'll be Coronet now," he said.

She nodded silently.

He went on: "I don't know you well, Missus French. I'm hoping you'll be more sensible than Bowie was about this fight between us. But hoping isn't trusting. I've seen too much of this to trust anyone on your side. That's been the trouble all along. None of us could trust anybody else."

Nola's eyes were on Craig. "Maybe there is someone in Coffin Gap that you will trust now."

MacQueen grinned broadly. "I'd believe Alan Craig now if he said the sun was the moon."

Without returning the smile, Nola nodded. "I'd trust him as far. I think most of the valley people do, too. If he's proved his neutrality to you, he certainly won't have any trouble with anybody else. As soon as you're better, Mister MacQueen, we all must get together. I hope a lot of problems have been solved today. If the pollution from this mountain does not stop, or at least is not controlled, it will mean the death of the valley, as much as that typhoid epidemic would have killed everyone if Alan had not been here to help us fight it and tell us what to do." Her body made a small, restless movement in the gloom. "I'd better go now. The rest of Coronet is on the way, and I'd like to stop them before they reach here. I don't think they'll have much heart left when they hear Bowie's dead."

Before she turned, her eyes settled on Craig for an instant. It was not a clearly defined expression. It rarely was in her. It lay just beneath the surface of that calm, Oriental quiescence. Craig came over and they embraced, deeply, passionately. Then she turned to pick her way out through the tunnel.

They watched her go. MacQueen was trembling with a gentle palsy.

"Hell, this mountain's almost played out anyway," he said. Then, drawing himself up, he turned to Daniels. "I think you can get me into the house all by yourself, if you put your mind to it. Don't you?"

Craig and Garnet followed them to the mouth of the adit, halting there. Craig told Daniels to bring the mountain wagon back for the bodies of Ingo and Bowie, after he had gotten MacQueen into the house. Then the cowhand helped MacQueen down the slope, leaving Garnet and Craig alone.

"The law will really want him now, won't it?" she asked.

"If he lives that long," Craig conceded.

Her chin lifted toward him. "I'm sorry for what happened in your office that time and almost happened again last night."

Craig sighed, and he could feel the small scar still, on his cheek burn in shame and embarrassment. "That's just it, Garnet. There's been a strong connection between Nola and me for a long time now, back even before I left Coffin Gap. I pushed it aside then, because I didn't want to think about it. I wanted to go to medical school. I wanted that more than anything else. Nola didn't think I would ever be coming back. For a time I wasn't sure myself. Then, when I did come back, I found her married to Bowie, and . . . and he had once been my best friend here. I thought my reason for holding back was because she was married, but Nola told me, after you left my office that day, that I was holding *myself* back. I'm not doing that any more."

"The time at Brockhalter's, when you kissed me . . . ?"

"I was very attracted to you, Garnet. I admit that. But I was also being dishonest with myself . . . and with you."

"That's what I wanted to know, Alan," she said then, reaching out briefly without making contact. Then her hand dropped to her side. "Here comes Daniels with the wagon. I've got to look after Dad."

She left him, finding her way alone down the slope. Craig stood, waiting for the mountain wagon to arrive, the gloom of the open adit gaping murkily behind him. The sun was shining brightly over his head now, and the cool, damp breeze that flowed down from the pristine heights above him seemed to lift his spirits. He felt a warm glow flow through him as he thought of Nola, and then a shudder as if from a great chill, not because they had found each other, but at how close they had come to having missed out altogether, to having passed each other one last time without having touched.

About the Author

Les Savage, Jr. was born in Alhambra, California, and grew up in Los Angeles. His first published story was "Bullets and Bullwhips" accepted by the prestigious magazine, Street & Smith's *Western Story*. Almost ninety more magazine stories followed, all set on the American frontier, many of them published in Fiction House magazines such as *Frontier Stories* and *Lariat Story Magazine* where Savage became a superstar with his name on many covers. His first novel, TREASURE OF THE BRASADA, appeared from Simon & Schuster in 1947. Due to his preference for historical accuracy, Savage often ran into problems with book editors in the 1950s who were concerned about marriages between his protagonists and women of different races — a commonplace on the real frontier but not in much Western fiction in that decade. Savage died young, at thirty-five, from complications arising out of hereditary diabetes and elevated cholesterol. Such noteworthy titles as SILVER STREET WOMAN, OUTLAW THICKETS, RETURN TO WARBOW, THE TRAIL, and BEYOND WIND RIVER have become classics of Western fiction. However, as a result of the censorship imposed on many of his works, only now are they being fully restored by returning to the author's original manuscripts. Among other recent restorations of Savage's great Western stories are FIRE DANCE AT SPIDER ROCK (Five Star Westerns, 1995), COPPER BLUFFS (Circle V Westerns, 1996), and MEDICINE WHEEL (Five Star Westerns, 1996). Much as Stephen Crane before him, while he wrote the shadow of his imminent death grew longer and longer across his young life, and he knew that, if he was going to do it at all, he would have to do it quickly. He did it well, better than almost anyone who wrote Western and frontier fiction, ever. Now that his novels and stories are being restored to what he had intended them to be, his achievement irradiated by his powerful and profoundly sensitive imagination will be with us always, as he had wanted it to be, as he had so rushed against time and mortality that it might be.

LES SAVAGE, JR.
MEDICINE WHEEL

Bob Hogarth arrives in Wyoming's Big Horn Basin with nothing but a small herd of cattle, the result of stubborn scraping and saving back in Texas. He is determined to do better, to own his own ranch, to become a man of substance. But there are lots of folks who aren't too eager to see Hogarth succeed, other ranchers with their own plans for the future, and a mysterious rustler on a barefoot horse. Nobody told Hogarth his dreams would come easy . . . but he knows they are worth fighting for.

___4444-7 $4.50 US/$5.50 CAN

COPPER BLUFFS

LES SAVAGE, JR.

Kenny Blacklaws returns to the East Texas town of Copper Bluffs nine years after the brutal murder of his stepfather, only to find himself smack dab in the middle of a war with cutthroat rustlers. But that isn't his only problem. His return also awakens the feelings of Corsica, the beautiful woman his stepbrother has claimed as his own. It's not long at all before just about everyone in Copper Bluffs is itching to see Kenny dead—just like his stepfather.

___4478-1 $4.50 US/$5.50 CAN

TROUBLE MAN

ED GORMAN

Ray Coyle used to be a gunfighter. And when he gets word his boy has been killed in a gunfight in Coopersville, he has to go there—to bring the body home. But when the old gunfighter steps off the train, he brings his gun with him, along with something else . . . trouble.

___4440-4 $4.99 US/$5.99 CAN

THE
MUSTANGERS
GARY McCARTHY

In Nevada in the early 1860s, an increasingly profitable trade is springing up. It is called mustanging—the breaking and selling of rogue horses to the highest bidder. When Pete Sills, an eager apprentice mustanger, signs on at the Cross T Ranch, all he wants is to learn the trade. But as soon as he meets Candy, the ranch owner's daughter, all that changes. Now he wants her. But to win her he first has to capture Sun Dancer, the fabulous palomino that Candy has her heart set on. And that means more trouble for Pete than he can ever imagine . . . and a lesson about pride and courage that he will never forget.

___4518-4 $3.99 US/$4.99 CAN

Dorchester Publishing Co., Inc.
P.O. Box 6640
Wayne, PA 19087-8640

NOBILITY

TIM McGUIRE

Clay Cole is a man on the run for a crime he never committed. But it's getting harder to run when it seems like everywhere he goes people have heard of the man known as the Rainmaker. When a young boy saves Clay's life, Clay figures the only honorable thing to do is help the boy's mother in the vicious land battle she's part of—even if that means staying put for a while. But if he stops running long enough for the past to catch up with him, the Rainmaker may not have much of a future.

___4526-5 $4.50 US/$5.50 CAN

Dorchester Publishing Co., Inc.
P.O. Box 6640
Wayne, PA 19087-8640

Please add $1.75 for shipping and handling for the first book and $.50 for each book thereafter. NY, NYC, and PA residents, please add appropriate sales tax. No cash, stamps, or C.O.D.s. All orders shipped within 6 weeks via postal service book rate. Canadian orders require $2.00 extra postage and must be paid in U.S. dollars through a U.S. banking facility.

Name_____
Address_____
City_____ State_____ Zip_____
I have enclosed $_____ in payment for the checked book(s).
Payment <u>must</u> accompany all orders. ❏ Please send a free catalog.
     CHECK OUT OUR WEBSITE! www.dorchesterpub.com

LAST OF
THE DUANES

Buck Duane's father was a gunfighter who died by the gun, and, in accepting a drunken bully's challenge, Duane finds himself forced into the life of an outlaw. He roams the dark trails of southwestern Texas, living in outlaw camps, until he meets the one woman who can help him overcome his past—a girl named Jennie Lee.

___4430-7 $4.99 US/$5.99 CAN

Dorchester Publishing Co., Inc.
P.O. Box 6640
Wayne, PA 19087-8640

Please add $1.75 for shipping and handling for the first book and $.50 for each book thereafter. NY, NYC, and PA residents, please add appropriate sales tax. No cash, stamps, or C.O.D.s. All orders shipped within 6 weeks via postal service book rate. Canadian orders require $2.00 extra postage and must be paid in U.S. dollars through a U.S. banking facility.

Name_____
Address_____
City_____State_____Zip_____
I have enclosed $_____ in payment for the checked book(s).
Payment <u>must</u> accompany all orders. ❑ Please send a free catalog.
CHECK OUT OUR WEBSITE! www.dorchesterpub.com

Last Chance

DEE MARVINE

Mattie Hamil is on a frantic journey west. On her own, with only her grit and determination to see her through, she has to find her charming gambler of a fiancé, and she has to do it fast—before her pregnancy shows. From a steamboat along the Missouri River to the rough-and-tumble post-gold-rush town of Last Chance, Montana, Mattie's trek leads her through danger and sorrow, friendship and joy. But even after she finds her fiancé, no bend in the trail leads to what she expected.

___4475-7 $4.99 US/$5.99 CAN

Dorchester Publishing Co., Inc.
P.O. Box 6640
Wayne, PA 19087-8640

Please add $1.75 for shipping and handling for the first book and $.50 for each book thereafter. NY, NYC, and PA residents, please add appropriate sales tax. No cash, stamps, or C.O.D.s. All orders shipped within 6 weeks via postal service book rate. Canadian orders require $2.00 extra postage and must be paid in U.S. dollars through a U.S. banking facility.

Name_____
Address_____
City_____ State_____ Zip_____
I have enclosed $_____ in payment for the checked book(s).
Payment <u>must</u> accompany all orders. ❏ Please send a free catalog.
    CHECK OUT OUR WEBSITE! www.dorchesterpub.com

THE CROSSING

By the Bestselling Author of *The Bear Paw Horses*

Jud is the son and grandson of famous Southern generals. He was reared in the genteel Virginia traditions of his widowed mother, but life on a Texas ranch has molded him in the harsh ways of the frontier. In the deadly Confederate campaign to secure the region, Jud sees brave men fall with their guns blazing or die from naked fear. But he is of better stock than most, and he'll be damned if he'll betray the land—and the woman—he loves just to save his own worthless hide.

_4084-0 $4.99 US/$5.99 CAN

POWDER RIVER

Gary McCarthy

Utah in the mid-1800s is truly wild, a land still largely untamed by law and settled by only the strongest—and bravest—souls. Few men have the courage to survive. And even fewer women. Despite the odds, Katie remains. A young, single woman, she is determined to raise her child and manage her sheep ranch without the help of any man...though a powerful cattleman, a ranch hand and an Eastern gentleman each have different ideas.

___4408-0 $5.50 US/$6.50 CAN

Dorchester Publishing Co., Inc.
P.O. Box 6640
Wayne, PA 19087-8640

Please add $1.75 for shipping and handling for the first book and $.50 for each book thereafter. NY, NYC, and PA residents, please add appropriate sales tax. No cash, stamps, or C.O.D.s. All orders shipped within 6 weeks via postal service book rate. Canadian orders require $2.00 extra postage and must be paid in U.S. dollars through a U.S. banking facility.

Name_____
Address_____
City_____State_____Zip_____
I have enclosed $_____ in payment for the checked book(s).
Payment __must__ accompany all orders. ❑ Please send a free catalog.
     CHECK OUT OUR WEBSITE! www.dorchesterpub.com